Virtuosity

Virtuosity

A Novel by Terry Bisson

Based on the Motion Picture Screenplay by Eric Bernt

POCKET BOOKS

New York   London   Toronto   Sydney   Tokyo   Singapore

This book is a work of fiction. Names, characters, places and incidents are products of the author's imagination or are used fictitiously. Any resemblance to actual events or locales or persons, living or dead, is entirely coincidental.

An *Original* Publication of POCKET BOOKS

POCKET BOOKS, a division of Simon & Schuster Inc.
1230 Avenue of the Americas, New York, NY 10020

Copyright © 1995 by Paramount Pictures Corporation

ISBN: 0-671-53752-0

First Pocket Books printing August 1995

10 9 8 7 6 5 4 3 2 1

POCKET and colophon are registered trademarks of Simon & Schuster Inc.

Printed in the U.S.A.

For Susan Ann Protter—
extraordinary agent and friend

Virtuosity

1

THE SUBWAY TRAIN PULLED INTO THE STATION. NEW train, new station. New people—they were all well-dressed, wearing clothes that had that just-pressed shine along the seams.

Two men pushed toward the door, making sure they would be first off the train. Two cops. LAPD poster boys: brand-new uniforms, regulation hair, regulation shoes, regulation steely jaws.

One white, one black. They might have been left-overs from a 1980s buddy movie, except that they didn't seem to be buddies. In fact, the lead cop, the African-American, didn't seem to notice the white cop at all as the doors opened and he pushed his way out of the subway car—jostling aside two or three commuters who stepped out of his way without looking at him, or at one another, or even at the identical *Los Angeles Times* in their hands.

"Century City. Watch your step. Have a nice day. The temperature upstairs is—"

Ignoring the perfect robotic conductor's voice, the

lead cop half ran across the platform to the UP escalator, stepping over and around a slow-moving mother and daughter with the smooth agility of a broken-field runner. The nameplate under his shield read: BARNES.

His partner was struggling to catch up. The nameplate under his shield read: DONOVAN. He was whining. "Barnes, man, wait up, give it a rest . . ." He was agile, too, but his was the reluctant agility of the follower.

Barnes didn't appear to hear. He was in his mid-thirties, with the narrow eyes of a prizefighter, the speed of a running back, and the white-heat intensity of a career urban policeman. All of which he exhibited as he wordlessly weaved his way up the steps, between the standees on the UP escalator. The standing commuters stepped back out of his way as if they did this every day; they seemed neither to notice nor to care that a police chase was underway.

"Barnes!"

Struggling to catch up, Donovan knocked over a man with a newspaper. He held out an apologetic hand, but the commuter was already getting up. Donovan shook his head and pressed on. "Barnes! 'Scuse me . . . 'scuse me . . . comin' through . . . police business . . . 'scuse me."

He caught up with him at the top. "Barnes, damn it! Ease off, man! Do you have any *actual* idea where you're *actually* going?"

Barnes spoke through gritted teeth without pausing or turning around. "Not until I get there."

The two men bolted off the escalator at the top, under the soaring glass-and-steel earthquake-resistant architecture of turn-of-the-century Los Angeles. Barnes was off again, weaving through the crowd, while Donovan followed, muttering under his breath.

"Fucking Dick Tracy!"

The sky overhead was the color of a TV set that has just been turned off. The sidewalk was crowded with commuters, all vaguely generic, all heading in the same direction, seeming neither to notice nor to care as the two officers bolted toward the street, through them, between and around them. Donovan knocked over another, a woman this time, and hesitated, wondering if he should stop to help her up, or . . .

He turned away from her and pressed on. "Barnes," he whined.

Behind him, the woman picked herself up wordlessly, brushing imaginary dirt off her perfect California clothing, and went on her way.

Barnes paused in front of a tall glass-and-steel building that soared into the shimmering gray sky.

WELLS FARGO PLAZA.

At a nearby newsstand, the rotating holographic head of a generic newscaster was publicizing the latest breaking story:

". . . and as LAPD officers gather evidence at this grisly crime scene, one can only ask oneself—what kind of lunatic would commit such unthinkable crimes? To find out, read today's . . ."

As it rotated in the air by the newsstand, the holographically projected head morphed sexually and racially into Hispanic, Asian, black, white, man, woman, young, old.

"The three adjectives which best describe this killer are sadistic, intelligent, and above all, dangerous . . ."

Donovan, out of breath, caught up. He grinned slightly, showing his youth. He stared at his partner, who wasn't smiling at all.

"Barnes, man, I cannot get over how different you look!"

Barnes shrugged. "Maybe it's the uniform." His

narrow eyes swept the crowd, the surrounding buildings—small shops, restaurants, coffee bars. Then he saw a sign directly across the plaza.

Underneath the words PLAZA SUSHI were a few Japanese characters, followed by a simple logo:

:)

Barnes reached down to his side and expertly unstrapped his gun, a matte-black regulation Glock nine mm.

Donovan worriedly, less confidently, did the same. "Did you see him? Where is he, Barnes?"

But Barnes was gone again, trotting across the crowded plaza and into the open front of the restaurant.

Donovan followed.

Most of the chic, well-dressed patrons were Euro-American, with a smattering of Asians. They sat at low, lacquered tables in elegant tatami-matted rooms, separated by rice paper and bamboo screens. The low, thudding beat of Eurasian technopop Muzak pulsed through the room. None of the diners looked up as the two policemen appeared in the doorway, guns drawn.

The hostess in a silk geisha gown also appeared imperturbed. "Good afternoon. Welcome to Plaza Sushi. May I help you?"

Barnes waved her to one side with the Glock and moved through the room, cubicle by cubicle, stopping to peer behind each of the delicate, beautifully detailed rice-paper partitions. The diners looked up from their black lacquer box-plates with mild curiosity, but no alarm.

"What do we look for?" asked Donovan, in a loud whisper.

"His eyes."

"What'll they look like?"

"Mine."

One of the diners was eating alone.

He sat behind a rice-paper screen near the back of the room. Although he was eating expertly with chopsticks and wearing a traditional Japanese kimono, he was Euro-American. A white guy in his mid-thirties. Almost a typical Hollywood glamour type. His hair was perfectly, almost too perfectly, tousled.

His sky-blue eyes gleamed like a new kind of metal. An unpleasant kind of metal.

Beside him on the floor was a zippered bowling-ball bag.

He wasn't wearing a nameplate, but if he had been, Barnes knew, it would have read: SID 6.7

Barnes saw the silhouette of Sid 6.7 through the rice-paper screen and motioned for Donovan to slip around to the rear. Donovan was only too glad to oblige.

Guns drawn, the two officers approached the lone diner's cubicle from different sides. Barnes from the front, Donovan from the rear.

Behind Barnes, the restaurant hostess was repeating, to no one in particular, "Good afternoon. Welcome to Plaza Sushi. Smoking or nonsmoking?"

Barnes crept soundlessly, closer and closer, across the wooden floor. He stopped right outside the entrance to the cubicle. From the back of the restaurant, Donovan watched with a look of mingled concern, amusement, and terror as Barnes lowered his Glock, aimed through the screen, and fired:

KRAK!

KRAK!

KRAK!

Sid 6.7 rolled to one side as the nine mm slugs splintered his table and sent his sushi flying. Grabbing his bowling-ball bag, he scrambled away, knocking over the screen between his cubicle and the next. The diners dove for cover, but quietly, almost listlessly.

No one screamed.

Sid 6.7 headed toward the back stairway, which led up to the second floor of the restaurant.

Donovan stepped out into the open, directly in his path. He raised his Glock nine mm, trying to remember if he had clicked the safety off. He had Sid 6.7 in his sights—until a woman stood up between them, wiping her mouth with a napkin, directly in his line of fire.

"Lady, move, you're . . ."

Grinning, his perfect teeth the color of new snow, Sid 6.7 stepped up behind the woman and reached around her with one arm, pinning her against his massive chest with the bowling-ball bag.

In his other hand he had a gun. It was huge and black: a .50 caliber Desert Eagle. Barely bothering to aim, he fired once:

BAROOM!

The explosion shook the walls. Bone and tissue flew in a fine spray. Donovan screamed in pain and grabbed his shattered arm.

"Ohmigod it hurts, it hurts too much—"

Still holding the woman, Sid 6.7 advanced toward Donovan. Then to one side and behind him, he saw Barnes advancing, ready to fire.

Hardly bothering to aim, Sid 6.7 fired once:

BAROOM!

The explosion shook the walls. Bone and tissue flew in a fine spray. Barnes grabbed his right arm, his shooting arm. His wound was identical to Donovan's—and so was the pain. It was white-hot, unexpected, excruciating.

As the Glock dropped from his fingers and he fell to his knees, Barnes saw Sid 6.7 advancing on Donovan, swinging the bowling-ball bag. The woman had been tossed aside and was getting to her feet, brushing imaginary dirt off her perfect California clothing.

With a sadistic grin, Sid 6.7 swung the bowling-ball bag in perfect time to the Muzak, hitting Donovan in the head, over and over.

"Ohmigod, ohmigod, Barnes, this is ohmigod . . ."

Donovan lay screaming, blood pumping out of his ruined arm into a pool on the varnished wood floor.

A pool that never got larger.

Barnes crawled toward his dropped gun. The pain in his arm was worse than any physical pain he had ever felt before. It was almost causing him to black out, billowing like a dark curtain over his mind, darkening his consciousness.

He forced it away with an effort of will.

"I've been shot before," he muttered, looking up angrily toward the ceiling. "This hurts worse than it should. Much worse!"

Still beating Donovan with the bowling-ball bag, Sid 6.7 raised the five-pound .50 caliber Desert Eagle and looked across the restaurant for Barnes, hidden behind a fallen rice-paper screen.

"I'm going to rehearse with your friend for a while," Sid 6.7 called out gaily, sticking his gun into the waistband of the jeans he wore under his kimono. He picked up Donovan with one hand, and the bowling-ball bag with the other. "I'll be back to perform a new piece with you!"

7

He raced up the narrow stairs to the second floor of the restaurant, carrying Donovan, who was now bleeding from both his head and his shattered arm.

With the Glock in his left hand, Parker fired twice after him:

KRAK!

KRAK!

No good. Missed.

Still bleeding, his right arm useless, Barnes stumbled toward the stairs.

The upstairs of Plaza Sushi was more open and sunny than the first floor. A long narrow room with low tables was dominated by a central bar behind a fish cooler, where three Japanese chefs wearing white coats and white paper hats expertly wielded knives, slicing and preparing sushi and sashimi delicacies.

Parker staggered up the stairs, still dripping blood from his shattered right arm. He looked around the room, at the diners who sat quietly eating, and at the three chefs who worked in the center of the room.

One of them had blue eyes the color of a new metal. It was Sid 6.7.

Barnes raised his Glock nine mm automatic. At the same instant, Sid 6.7 set down his knife and grabbed the chef to his right, pulling him in front of his body as a shield.

The hostage chef looked dazed but remarkably undisturbed by this break in his routine. The other chefs looked up curiously and then kept on slicing fish.

Sid 6.7 raised his Desert Eagle to the side of the Japanese chef's head.

"Where's Donovan?" Barnes asked. His eyes were cold, as cold as the eyes of the quarry he faced.

"Your partner? Performing his solo." Sid 6.7 grinned. "You can be next."

Barnes didn't return the smile. Instead he raised his left arm and fired:

KRAK!

KRAK!

The bullets went straight through the chest of the innocent Japanese chef and into the chest of Sid 6.7.

Looking more bemused than ever, the chef slumped to the floor. Sid 6.7 dropped him and backed away, looking down at the two holes in his chest and then up at Barnes in disbelief.

A smile began to play across Sid 6.7's shining, handsome features as he watched Barnes advance toward him across the room, stepping between the patrons who moved, slowly and serenely, out of his way.

Barnes fired again:

KRAK!

KRAK!

KRAK!

Barnes watched with satisfaction as blood pumped from the holes in Sid 6.7's chest and shoulder, streaming down his legs, dripping from his fingers.

Sid 6.7's shattered arm hung useless. As his five-pound pistol dropped and crashed to the floor, he smiled with admiration. "You're *insane!*"

Barnes fired twice more into Sid 6.7's chest.

KRAK!

KRAK!

Then the Glock clicked, twice.

"And the violin has no strings," said Sid 6.7, as he dropped out of sight behind the cooler, onto the blood-drenched floor.

Barnes advanced, grimacing with the incredible, indescribable, unexpected pain in his arm as he switched the Glock to his right hand and jammed a new clip into it.

Then he saw the bowling-ball bag on the sushi bar where Sid 6.7 had dropped it.

It was leaking blood through the zipper.

Whatever was in there, it was *not* a bowling ball.

Barnes looked down, through the glass top of the cooler. Donovan lay stretched out full-length inside. He was convulsing up and down, in slow motion; he would have been screaming if his mouth hadn't been bound with duct tape.

Donovan's hands were also bound, with bare wire, which was spitting sparks into the frosty air of the cooler as he frantically tried to pull them loose.

He was being electrocuted.

"What the hell!" Barnes raised the lid of the cooler and, ignoring the electric shock ripping through his own body, tore the wires loose from Donovan's hands.

But not in time.

"Shit! What the hell is this? You're cheating . . ."

Barnes leaned over and looked behind the freezer, firing twice, three times down:

KRAK!

KRAK!

KRAK!

But the bullets just splintered the varnished floor. Sid 6.7 was gone. So was his Desert Eagle.

Even the blood was gone.

"You cheated!" Barnes said, then gagged as he was grabbed by the throat from behind. It was Sid 6.7, who had somehow gotten around him, behind him. He pushed Barnes across the room and jammed him up against the wall, holding him there by the neck.

"I have a new piece, just for you," Sid 6.7 said. "It's called, 'First You Suffer, Then You Die.'"

"You cheated!" Barnes managed to choke out.

"It's a ragtime thing," said Sid 6.7 with a dazzling smile as he began to tighten his grip, waiting to feel the satisfying snap of cartilage breaking under his fingers.

Then his smile faded. Barnes himself was fading, dematerializing from within Sid 6.7's grasp.

"Wait!" Sid 6.7 shouted angrily, looking up toward the ceiling. "You can't take him yet. I'm not finished!"

But Barnes was gone. Sid 6.7 looked down at his own body, and he saw the blood beginning to flow back *into* the holes in his chest. His shoulder was healing itself, like a stop-action film in reverse.

He looked into the cooler. Donovan was also gone.

The sushi chef who had been shot was standing up, going back to work, good as new.

Sid 6.7 shook his head with disgust and spat onto the beautifully varnished floor. "Bureaucrats!"

2

UNDER THE HIGH-FREQUENCY, HIGH-TECH HUM OF THE floor-to-ceiling big-screen monitors, and over the unhearable, high-tech quantum howl of the silicon chips powering the VR displays, a low-tech whine was heard in the top-secret inner sanctum of the LETAC (Law Enforcement Technology Advancement Center) experimental Virtual Reality laboratory.

An old-fashioned whine. A mechanical whine.

An actual physical movement was taking place: something more substantial than electrons was being moved from place to place.

Meat.

Two men in skeletal aluminum pods were being lowered from the ceiling to the concrete floor by two electrical robotic arms.

The pods reached floor level and the robotic arms retracted. Both men wore bright orange coveralls and white plastic helmets connected by cables to the banks of computers that lined the walls of the lab.

One man was black, one white. Both looked dead.

The tops of the pods slid to one side. The helmets

retracted, revealing polyurethane skull caps, from which silver acupuncture needles extruded, giving each man the look of the Hellraiser in an old movie.

On the wall behind the two men, over the computer banks and below the monitors, a liquid crystal display read:

VIRTUAL REALITY CRIMINAL INVESTIGATION SIMULATOR
Simulation: TERMINATED.
Duration: 2 hours, 42 min, 11.65 sec.
3:04:32 PM, March 12, 1999

Five people rushed into the lab from the glassed-in control booth.

"What's going on?" asked Elizabeth Deane. "Why are we stopping?" She spoke like a woman who was used to getting answers, which, as the President's "Crime Czar," in charge of federal crime-control funding, she was. "Frederick?" she demanded sharply.

"Just a glitch," said Fred Wallace. He stuck his nervous hands into his pockets. He knew his hands gave him away. He had learned to keep them under the table at board meetings, to give the impression that the CEO of LETAC was unflappable; but here there was no table to hide them under.

William Cochran, the Los Angeles Police Chief, wasn't nervous. He was furious. "Get those fucking caps off those men!" he shouted. He looked around the room wildly. "Where's a medic?"

The youngest person in the room seemed the calmest. Dr. Madison Carter picked up a wall phone, and in a soft, feminine voice, she said, "Paramedics. Please."

A tall gaunt figure emerged from the shadows. It was Daryl Lindenmeyer, the designer of the software. His gray hair was combed over his bald spot, and he was skinny and stooped, as if he were always looking for a dropped contact lens, which was ironic, since his eyes were magnified by thick spectacles. He rushed toward the two pods, shouting:

"Stay away from the VR pods. I have this under control!"

Two paramedics ran into the lab. They looked to Fred Wallace, who gave them a curt nod, then rushed toward the two men in the pods, brushing Lindenmeyer aside.

The black man was sitting up, looking dazed. The white man was thrashing his arms and legs, as if in a seizure. He began to scream.

The man sitting up was Parker Barnes. He was a different Barnes than the Barnes in the Virtual Reality simulation. His was the same face, but harder, with narrower eyes and deeper lines. Instead of a starched, new blue LAPD uniform, he wore orange prison coveralls. And in his left ear he wore an earring, a gold stud.

Barnes looked down at the screaming Donovan, apparently unmoved by his so-called partner's suffering. Then he looked at Lindenmeyer.

"There's a problem," he said. "There's a big problem over here."

Dr. Madison Carter ran across the room with the two paramedics. She helped one of them hold down Donovan's flailing arms and legs, while the other one prepared an injection. She shook her head, muttering, "He's going into shock . . ."

Meanwhile, a familiar face stared out from the big-screen monitor on the wall. Blond hair, blue eyes like a new kind of metal.

Under the monitor, a row of CD-size cartridge modules protruded from slots in the main VR console. Each was identified by a name on a tape:

SHEILA 1.7
SUSHI CHEF 1.3
SUSHI CHEF 1.3
GEISHA HOSTESS 3.2
SID 6.7
DINER 1.4
DINER 1.4

Sid 6.7 on the big-screen monitor no longer wore a chef's hat or a kimono; he wore nondescript jeans and a T-shirt that read:

CRIME IS THE QUESTION.
LETAC IS THE ANSWER.

Behind him, the sushi restaurant had apparently returned to normal: diners ate, chefs sliced and diced, Muzak throbbed.

Sid 6.7 turned and walked down the narrow stairs behind him, into the bottom floor of the restaurant.

Elizabeth Deane and Fred Wallace stood back, watching the paramedics. "What's wrong with that man?" Deane demanded. "I thought you said there was no danger?"

"The sensitivity calibrations must have slipped," said the LETAC CEO. He attempted what he imagined was a casual shrug. "Just a tad."

"You call *that* a *tad?*"

Donovan had gone rigid. The paramedics had taken him out of the pod and placed him on a stretcher; they were attempting to get his heart started with an electrical fibrillating device.

THUMP

THUMP

15

Again and again. But no success.

Parker Barnes looked on dazedly, dispassionately. "I'm cold," he said to no one in particular.

Madison Carter stepped back from the stretcher. She had seen death before, but this . . .

She looked up at the big-screen monitor on the wall. Sid 6.7 was walking through the lobby of the sushi restaurant.

There was a painting on the wall of the restaurant, a desert scene. Sid 6.7 walked toward it, and *into* it. Suddenly Sid 6.7 was walking through the desert landscape that had been in the painting. Another painting hung in the air near him, like a leftover part from a Salvador Dali masterpiece.

It was a painting of the interior of a Japanese restaurant.

Carter shivered. It was too creepy. She looked back just in time to see one of the paramedics pulling a sheet over Donovan's face. Even though he wore a convict's orange coveralls, in death he seemed no more than a boy.

Daryl Lindenmeyer preferred to communicate by e-mail because it meant he didn't have to reveal his appearance, which was less than impressive, or rely on his voice, which was pitched a bit too high to be reliably effective. Person-to-person contact was clumsy at best; nevertheless, it was sometimes essential, so he tried to muster his most soothing and convincing tones as he drove the electrical cart through the storage rooms to the front gate.

His passengers, Elizabeth Deane and Fred Wallace, rode in the back seat of the modified golf cart, which was used to provide VIP transportation through

LETAC's vast complex of storerooms, labs, and offices.

"We use neural primes to tap right into the brain," Lindenmeyer was explaining.

"You mean those acupuncture-needle-type things?" Deane asked.

"Correct. They tap directly into the neural centers of the brain. Therefore, if the simulator isn't calibrated absolutely correctly, experiencing death at this high level of Virtual Reality can, uh, well . . ."

There must be a good way to say it! Lindenmeyer wished he were online, where he could use a symbol, an IMHO, or even a smileyface to help lessen the shock. Direct, naked, animal speech was such a primitive method.

"Well *what?*" Elizabeth Deane was sounding distinctly unsympathetic.

"It can be like experiencing death within a dream. You know? The experience becomes, well, like, real."

Deane was not impressed. She ignored Lindenmeyer and spoke directly to Wallace. He was, after all, the man in charge of LETAC—the man to whom, or at least through whom, the President's Commission on Crime was funneling billions in grants and contracts.

"How did this happen, Fred?" she asked coldly.

"It shouldn't have happened!" Wallace said, his voice rising to a whine. He turned to Lindenmeyer: "There were supposed to be fail-safes built into the system."

"There were," protested Lindenmeyer. "I even installed backups to the fail-safes!"

He squinted as the cart hummed out the last doorway, through a loading-dock area, and into the parking lot. The direct sunlight gave Lindenmeyer an instant headache. He hated the outside. Virtual Reality was so much easier to control; it had better skies, less heat, less pollution.

"Well, something went wrong!" insisted Wallace.

"Somebody's obviously been screwing with my program," muttered Lindenmeyer.

He stopped the cart by a waiting limousine. The driver had already gotten out and was holding open the rear door.

"The assignment was clear and unambiguous," said Deane. The springs of the golf cart squeaked as she lifted her bulk off the seat and stepped down to the pavement. "It was to give my law-enforcement people realistic, dangerous scenarios in which to practice, while protecting them from real world risks. From my perspective, it's a complete failure."

"Mrs. Deane, please!" protested Wallace. "None of your people were hurt. The whole reason we used convict volunteers was to ferret out any glitches in the system during this development and testing phase." He got out of the cart and followed her toward the limousine. "The issue here shouldn't be whether or not a convicted criminal died. You and the Commission on Crime pay me and LETAC for results. Not for how I get you there."

But Elizabeth Deane wasn't waiting around to hear any more. As she ducked her massive gray-crowned head to get into the limousine, she said, "Mr. Wallace, I believe I'll be telling the President we've just wasted 3.7 billion—that's *billion!*—dollars developing a cruel and convoluted way to control our prison population. By killing them off in Virtual Reality simulations."

Wallace followed her into the rear seat, pleading, "Elizabeth, please try and consider the bigger picture . . ."

The limo driver slammed the door on the CEO's words, and Lindenmeyer floored the pedal on the cart, making a U-turn back toward the familiar, comforting darkness of LETAC's labyrinthine maze of storage rooms and conference rooms, offices and labs.

"Bureaucrats!" he muttered as he drove.

3

I'M SORRY, PARKER."

Police Chief Cochran was helping Parker Barnes out of the pod that had cradled his body during his insertion into Virtual Reality.

Barnes's arm was still throbbing from the incredible pain of the gunshot wound. "Sorry?" he asked.

"About what happened to Donovan. About what happened to you. This has never happened before. They told me that—"

"Told you?" Barnes was wobbly. He bent over with hands on knees, shaking his head. "You trust too much, Billy."

Then he straightened up and attempted a smile, touching the older man's shoulder reassuringly. "Don't sweat it. For me, anyway, it was just a—"

He broke off suddenly. His face went cold again, hard, as if a shield had been lowered over it.

A uniformed prison guard was approaching. He was carrying a belly band, chains, handcuffs, and shackles. They clanked and rattled menacingly as he crossed the dark lab toward Parker Barnes and Police Chief Cochran.

Barnes stood motionless, resigned, as the officer strapped the heavy leather belt around his waist, then locked his handcuffed wrists to it.

Barnes knew the drill.

Cochran watched with pain in his eyes. "It was good seeing you back in uniform, Parker," he said. "Even if it was only VR."

Instead of answering, Barnes said, "He cheated."

"What? Who cheated?"

"Sid 6.7. LETAC's creation. Electrocution wasn't on his methods-of menu."

"What the fuck are you talking about, Parker? Methods of what?"

The prison guard finished shackling Barnes's ankles, then straightened up and stepped away.

"Methods of killing," Barnes said. "Handgun, automatic rifle, shotgun, knife, blunt objects. His hands. His teeth. His *head,* even. But electrocution was not an available option."

"How do you know?" Cochran asked.

"Because I cheated, too. I checked the database while you were all sitting around on your asses waiting for Crime Queen Deane. Here, I'll show you . . ."

Chains clanking, Barnes shuffled toward the nearest keyboard at the monitoring station. Just as he was about to strike the keys, a door slammed and a voice was heard from the darkness.

"Hey!"

It was Lindenmeyer, striding into the room, his thin hair flying loose.

"Whoa! Get away from that keyboard! You there, don't let that convict touch anything, or—"

Cochran stepped forward to pull Barnes back out of

the way, but too late. Lindenmeyer had already pushed him. Barnes, his legs hampered by the shackles, fell backward; he would have hit the floor if he hadn't been caught by Police Chief Cochran.

Barnes stood, slowly, helped to his feet by Cochran, his expression unchanged, still a blank.

Then he lunged at Lindenmeyer.

"Hey! Help! Aaaahhhhh!" screamed Lindenmeyer. "Don't touch me! Don't let him touch me!"

Cochran reached in and grabbed Barnes's arm. "Parker!"

The prison guard who had chained Barnes was joined by another who had waited by the door; they both rushed over and helped pull Barnes off the flailing, screaming Lindenmeyer. One of the guards had his club pulled, and was about to lower it on Barnes's head, when he felt a hand stop him.

He looked back over his shoulder.

"Enough."

It was the chief of police.

He lowered the club, and the two guards hustled Barnes off toward the door, his clinking chains loud in the soft humming darkness of the computer lab.

Lindenmeyer sat on the floor, rubbing his arm and then the side of his face. "That convict assaulted me!" he screamed at Police Chief Cochran. "I want to press charges."

Cochran shook his head and laughed. "Charges? That was Parker Barnes. Any charges you could add wouldn't mean much to him."

Cochran made no move to help the LETAC programmer to his feet. Instead, he followed the guards and Barnes out the door.

"You're not helping me any, Parker," Cochran said. The chief was walking beside Barnes and the guards, toward the prison transport van in LETAC's rear parking lot. Cochran had to slow his pace to match Barnes's chained shuffle. "I'm doing everything I can to get you out of the hole, and you keep fucking up."

"Did you bring my stuff?" Barnes asked.

Cochran shook his head in amazement. "I get you nine months off your sentence for volunteering for this experiment, and all you care about is a few pieces of colored chalk!"

"Time off won't help me for another seventeen years," said Barnes. "Chalk I can use right now."

They were at the prison transport van. While one guard unlocked the rear door, and another held Barnes by the short chain attached to the rear of his belly band, Cochran asked, "You shot the sushi chef, Parker. You shot the sushi chef *twice!* What the hell did you have to shoot an innocent bystander for?"

Barnes shrugged, his eyes narrowed against the fierce afternoon sun. "He wasn't real."

"So what! You were supposed to pretend he was."

"And pretend to die? Like Donovan?"

The door of the prison van was open. Barnes climbed in. It was a cold windowless box with two metal benches, one along each wall. He sat down and looked out at Cochran.

"You got your guinea pig, now I want my chalk. That's what's real here, Billy."

Cochran shook his head in exasperation. "Pull it together or you're going to pull yourself down."

Barnes nodded. His face softened just a little. "You're the only one I got left. My only link."

Cochran reached in and touched the younger man on the arm. "I'll be by next Tuesday."

"I'll be there," said Barnes. "I'm not going anywhere."

The door slammed shut. The interior of the van was

thrown into near darkness. The only light came from a four-by-four-inch slot at the front, covered with steel mesh.

As the prison van's engine started, a guard's face appeared behind the mesh. Dark, almost friendly.

"Yo, Parker. Think Big Red's gonna freak when you come back without his girlfriend?"

Parker Barnes didn't answer. Instead he sat in silence as the van hurtled forward, the only sound the occasional clinking of his chains.

4

SID 6.7 WAS IN HIS SID SANDBOX.

On the big-screen monitor high on the wall of the LETAC's VR lab, and on a half-dozen smaller monitors scattered around the room, he stood in the desert, casually but neatly dressed in Desert Storm camouflage and campaign cap.

The sky above Sid 6.7 was the same brilliant metallic blue as his eyes. A grand piano was behind him, half buried in a dune. At one side of him there was a water fountain, tilted in the sand, and at the other, a glass and aluminum phone booth. A buzzard sat on top of the phone booth, dozing. Lindenmeyer, who had created both Sid and his Sid Sandbox, was nothing if not playful.

But Sid 6.7 wasn't interested in his playthings. He stared thoughtfully at the screen, as if he could see out of it, through it, into Lindenmeyer's dark VR lab. His blue eyes were shining as if with tears, and he seemed almost to be pouting.

"You're in me, aren't you, Daryl?" he asked.

"In you?"

Lindenmeyer was in the center of the lab, typing furiously into a keyboard under a small monitor covered with scrolling binary code.

"Your personality. Your past. You're part of my profile, aren't you?"

Lindenmeyer didn't bother to answer Sid 6.7's question; he had other things on his mind. "Electrocution is *not* part of your methods-of menu."

Sid 6.7 shrugged theatrically. "I tinkered with it. You gave me the power to do that, and inmate Barnes was going to *kill* me."

Lindenmeyer toggled a function key and the binary code disappeared. Sid 6.7 appeared on his small monitor, as well as on the others.

Lindenmeyer looked at Sid 6.7 thoughtfully. "He scared you!"

"Not losing is the universal override," responded Sid 6.7.

"But I wouldn't have let him win," said Lindenmeyer. "You can't give away so much, you have to stay within the limits of the simulation—"

Sid 6.7's blue eyes were confused. "Oh, but I have all these vague, deeply contradictory urges, Daryl—memories that surface when I play this piano you gave me. Rejection and acne. Sublime virtuosity—a sense of profound opportunity, as if some magnificent future awaits me—always followed by humiliation and shame. Crushing, unjust—"

"Those are pseudo-emotions generated by a personal history grid I put in your personality program," interrupted Lindenmeyer.

"Your history, Daryl?"

Lindenmeyer didn't respond, but the answer was obvious. He was relieved when Wallace entered the room.

Just as Sid 6.7 deferred to Lindenmeyer, his creator, Lindenmeyer deferred to Fred Wallace, who in a

26

sense had created him. At least he had given him the budget and the creative freedom to bring his dream to life. "What's up, Mr. Wallace?"

"What's *up*?" Wallace closed the cellular phone he was carrying, folding it and replacing it into the lapel pocket of his expensive suit. "The Crime Czar—Mrs. Deane—she's flipping out over this death thing, that's what's up!"

Lindenmeyer shrugged and went back to his keyboard. Sid 6.7 was replaced by the scrolling lines of code. "I think Carl Reilly has been screwing with my software—the calibrations, some of the options menus. The problem with the simulator is that it's working *too* well."

"The *problem* . . ." Wallace began; then he decided to cut directly to the chase. "I have no choice but to pull the plug on the VR simulator project, Daryl."

Lindenmeyer groaned as if he had been struck. "But . . ."

Fred Wallace softened his tone. "The problem is, Daryl, we've been wasting your programming brilliance on Virtual beings like Sid what's-his-name."

"Sid 6.7," said Lindenmeyer. On the big-screen monitor high on the wall, Sid 6.7 stood in his Sid Sandbox, looking at the screen as if worried and fascinated at the same time.

"Sid 6.7 then. Virtual Reality is a waste of time, Daryl. Genius like yours needs to be applied in the real world."

"The real world?" Lindenmeyer suddenly realized where the conversation was going, and he tried to head it off. "No way I'm working under a hardware twerp like Carl Reilly, Mr. Wallace."

"Hardware is only as good as the software that runs it, Daryl. You told me that yourself."

"Damn right," said Lindenmeyer, going back to his keyboard.

"It's no coincidence that Reilly's been working with your module protocol, Daryl."

Lindenmeyer waited, his hands poised over the keyboard. He both dreaded and wanted to hear what came next. But the LETAC CEO was finished, heading toward the door.

"Mr. Wallace?"

Wallace turned, looking toward Lindenmeyer. Then he realized that it wasn't Lindenmeyer who had spoken. Both men looked up toward the big-screen monitor, where Sid 6.7 stood in front of his piano in the dunes.

Wallace looked from the screen to Lindenmeyer; panic edged his voice. "How does he know who I am?"

Lindenmeyer shrugged, pointing into the darkness. "Mikes. Video cameras. He hears, sees, everything."

"Mr. Wallace." Sid 6.7 had taken off his campaign cap. He looked polite, almost respectful. "You're really going to shut me down?" he asked.

Wallace glared at Lindenmeyer, then glared at Sid 6.7. "Yes, I am."

He turned on his heel and walked out of the circle of light, into the darkness toward the door.

Sid 6.7 also turned. He held out his hand and made a flipping motion with his thumb, tossing an imaginary coin. And a coin appeared at the top of its arc and fell, shining, back into his palm.

Sid 6.7 walked into the phone booth beside him, shut the door, and dialed a number. The buzzard woke briefly, then went back to sleep.

Lindenmeyer watched with an amazement that was almost love.

And what should he love, he wondered, if not his own creation?

* * *

28

At the side door of LETAC's vast suburban complex, Fred Wallace emerged into the daylight just as his cellular phone rang, muffled in his suit pocket.

He shut the door behind him. He pulled the phone from his pocket and unfolded it.

"Wallace here."

The voice through the phone was unmistakable. "Newsflash: you're not the boss, Fred. Not anymore."

There was a *click*.

Wallace folded his phone and walked off, looking for his car, his amazement tinged not with love but with fear.

5

A DOOR SLIDES OPEN.

A voice says, "Step forward."

A man steps through.

A door slides shut.

That's prison life in a nutshell. Doors without handles, voices without faces. Life without choice, without hope, without warmth or color.

Cold.

Gray.

The color of steel.

The color of time.

Parker Barnes, convict 673429, was returned to the L.A. County Maximum Security Facility through the rear door, where his chains were removed by the two guards who had escorted him to LETAC's Virtual Reality lab. Then he was passed without seeing another human face through a series of short locked hallways into the one-man, coffinlike elevator that ran to the top maxi-maxi tiers.

The elevator door slid open, revealing a small room with a steel bench.

"Step forward."

Barnes stepped forward.

The door slid shut behind him.

"Strip."

An overhead video surveillance turret whined as Barnes stripped, then stood naked, arms held out to the sides. He knew the drill.

Another turret whined, and the red crescent of a laser scan ran over every inch of Barnes's body, pausing on the long scar that circled his left arm just below the elbow. That scar always confused the scanner.

"Open mouth."

The laser scanned his teeth.

"Bend over."

His buttocks.

"Spread 'em."

Parker Barnes knew the drill. He performed it like an automaton.

A door slid open.

"Step forward."

Parker Barnes stepped forward.

The door slid shut behind him.

He was in another, even smaller room, this one with four steel doors. A plastic bag lay in the center of the room.

Barnes opened the bag and took out a clean orange prison uniform. He put it on.

A stenciled sign on the door he had just come through read:

STRIP SEARCH

Identical stenciled signs on the three other doors read:

HOSPITAL BLOCK
MAIN CELL BLOCK
ISOLATION BLOCK

Barnes stood in front of the ISOLATION BLOCK doorway, waiting for it to slide open. Instead, to his left, the MAIN CELL BLOCK door began to slide open.

For the first time since leaving Police Chief Cochran, Parker Barnes's face showed expression.

The expression was alarm.

"Wrong door, asshole!" he called out to the ceiling.

The door was opening very slowly. Through the tiny four-by-four-inch mesh-covered window, Parker could see movement, which resolved itself into a blur of hair and flesh, which resolved itself into a bare chest, approaching—then a watery slate-gray eye at the window.

The shouts from inside the cell block echoed through the opening door:

"Get him, Red! Go, Big Red!"

Parker Barnes realized what was happening. He lunged.

Inside the cell block, the noise was deafening as the caged men on two tiers of Main watched their favorite swagger toward the opening door.

Few of the prisoners liked Big Red, and fewer still knew the man he had been swearing all day, through oaths and tears, to kill, ever since the news came back that Donovan had died in the LETAC experiment. But it wasn't hard for the prisoners on Main to figure out which side they were on.

Parker Barnes had been a cop, after all. Once a cop, always a cop.

So when the guards "mistakenly" left Big Red's cell door open and "mistakenly" opened the wrong door for the arriving prisoner, the men all knew they were in for a good show.

Big Red was stripped to his shorts, and anyone who thought that he was a sissy just because he liked men was in for a rude and painful awakening. Red was all scars, tattoos and muscles, the product of a prison weight room and a jailhouse tattoo artist.

The guards in the central control station pretended not to notice as Big Red approached the opening door, and bent down to peer through and taunt his victim.

Big Red was expecting to see another eye, a worried eye.

Big Red wasn't expecting the steel fist that crashed through a quarter-inch of glass-and-steel mesh to slam against his eye socket with the nasty satisfying crunch of steel and glass and bone.

"All right!" The cheer went up from the cells on the tier. The cheers turned to jeers, and even the guards dropped their pretense of inattention and began to watch openly.

Big Red staggered backward, reeling, clutching his ruined eye as the door slid open.

While the door continued to open, Parker Barnes looked down at his left hand, evaluating the damage. He used his teeth to pull the shards of glass from his knuckles. Under the ripped skin, steel was visible. On his palm there was a tattoo:

Wentlow™ Model 17-L.

The door was open.

"Kill him, Red! Tear him apart!"

Parker looked up from his hand. Red was on his feet.

Parker spit out the glass onto the metal floor.

Red got his balance, raised a giant fist.

And again, Parker lunged, this time through the open door.

The fight raged for almost twenty minutes, up and down the hallway below the tiers of cells on Main.

The men cheered and four armed guards looked on from their stations along the walls.

Soon the floor was slick with blood, and the blood was not just Big Red's. Though Parker Barnes's left arm couldn't bleed, his nose and face could bleed; his neck and teeth and ears could bleed; so could his other arm, his right fist, not to mention his thigh which had the tooth marks of the half-man, half-beast he was battling.

Big Red was a tornado of grief and rage, almost unstoppable. The physical pain that Barnes inflicted on him mattered little, compared with the pain of his loss; and he was fueled with rage, a rage that Barnes didn't feel, couldn't feel, even as he slammed Big Red up against the bars of the cells, even as he fought back with tooth and nail and hand and foot.

Parker Barnes knew rage: it was his most intimate companion, the familiar of his days, the leman of his nights; but it was not a rage against this man. Whatever Big Red had done in the past, whatever had gotten him into prison, now he was simply a victim. Like Barnes himself.

"Get him, Big Red!" the prisoners cried from the tiers.

Barnes tried to pull away, to scramble up the stairs to the second level, but Big Red yanked him down, then started hammering him with a huge fist. Barnes twisted his head away and let Big Red's fist shatter itself against the corrugated metal step.

"Kill him!" shouted the prisoners from the tiers.

Howling with pain, Big Red fell backward—and Barnes was on top of him. The two rolled down the short flight of stairs; at the bottom, Big Red was on top. He bared his teeth and howled with the anticipation of the kill. Desperate, Barnes went for Big Red's remaining eye with long, slender steel fingers.

Big Red ducked and grabbed at Barnes's prosthetic left arm, trying to wrench it off. Grimacing with pain, Barnes pulled free and wrapped the arm around Red's throat, just as Sid 6.7 had wrapped his arm around the throat of the Japanese chef in the VR restaurant.

Only Big Red was not a hostage but an enemy. A deadly enemy.

Big Red screamed, then stopped screaming as Barnes's grip tightened. Barnes had found his rage—or rather, it had found him. It swept over him like a dark flood.

Big Red's remaining eye began to bulge out, and his fist struck the air ineffectually.

"Kill him, Barnes!" the prisoners shouted down from the cells. As the balance of power had shifted in the fight, so had their less-than-enduring loyalties.

"That's enough!"

Barnes felt the cold wood of a billy club against his own neck. "That's it. Break it up."

"Kill!" shouted the men. *Kill!* murmured Parker Barnes's own rage, fueled by all the injustices he had endured, the horrors he had seen. *Kill . . .*

He squeezed tighter, watching Big Red's beefy face turn from red to blue, even as Barnes's own world darkened around him. . . .

Parker Barnes awoke in a narrow, dark, familiar cell. His throat and hands were sore. Every part of his body was aching. His orange coveralls were stained with blood.

His own and Big Red's.

He wondered how his adversary was faring. Then he stopped wondering. What did it matter?

A narrow slot in the steel door slid open, and a tray was pushed through. On it was a repair kit—a plastic dish of ready-mixed epoxy, a wooden applicator, a piece of sandpaper.

"Where's my chalk?" Barnes shouted. "Cochran promised he'd get me my chalk!"

The slot slid closed. Nothing but silence followed.

Resignedly, Barnes troweled the epoxy onto his ruined knuckles with the applicator. It was a little light against his dark "skin," but it was almost a match. It set up immediately and he began sanding his knuckles smooth.

The slot opened again and another tray slid through. On it was a small plastic bag containing pieces of colored chalk.

Parker Barnes picked it up with a look of almost satisfaction.

6

AS MUCH AS FRED WALLACE COMPLAINED ABOUT Elizabeth Deane (and he loved to complain about Elizabeth Deane), dealing with her and the other government bureaucrats he depended on for funding wasn't the hardest part of his job as CEO of LETAC. The hardest part was stroking and coddling the unwashed computer nerds and nanotech neurotics he depended on for technical innovations. Nerds and neurotics like Lindenmeyer and Reilly, who never went out of the house, had no taste in clothes, neither drank nor smoked, didn't care about women or money or fame. They were pure ego; they were like artists or monks, unfathomable.

But stroked and coddled they had to be; so Wallace resisted the urge to throw Carl Reilly off the catwalk as he walked him through LETAC's cavernous central section, toward the nanotech lab.

Reilly was a little less than thirty years old, and he weighed a little less than three hundred pounds. His long hair was tied back in a greasy ponytail, and he wore drip-dry pants and a drip-dry shirt, with a plastic pen holder bursting with pens, and a button that read as follows:

SOFTWARE ISN'T HARD.

Fred Wallace tried to keep the loathing and impatience out of his voice as he explained his plans, and he listened to Reilly's objections with what he hoped was a passable counterfeit of fatherly interest.

"I know Lindenmeyer's done *some* good work," Reilly complained. "But . . ."

Wallace put his hand on Reilly's pudgy arm. "Carl, you've got to admit the personality structures in his character modules are uniquely dynamic."

Reilly pouted. "I guess. But overall, Mr. Wallace, Daryl and I are not what I consider to be in the same league."

They paused at a marked door:

NANOTECH LAB
NO ENTRY
THIS MEANS YOU

While Reilly fumbled for the key, Wallace tried his most soothing tones. "The same league? Of course not. No one is saying that, Carl."

Reilly opened the door and, remembering himself, let his boss walk through first, then switched on the lights.

They were in a giant two-story room, on a catwalk overlooking big vats and surgical tables.

"All I'm saying," Reilly said, "is that I don't need Lindenmeyer's help."

"Carl," said Wallace patiently, "you are the most brilliant individual LETAC has ever worked with. But your expertise is hardware, not software."

Reilly turned toward Wallace. "Am I getting Daryl's budget?"

"Absolutely," said Wallace, relaxing. The battle was won. "Carl, your nanotechnology represents the cutting edge, and LETAC needs that edge."

He put his arm around the young man's fat shoulders—not without a slight shudder of loathing—and walked with him down the creaking steel stairs from the catwalk, through the pools of darkness into a shadowy central area, where giant soft plastic bags that looked like entrails hung from the ceiling, interconnected with tubes and wires.

In the bags were shapes that might have been animal, might have been human, might have been both or neither.

"But I will require a certain accountability, from time to time," Wallace said. "The Crime Queen needs to be reassured that the public's money is well spent."

Reilly looked insulted, then began to swell with his own importance. "Well spent?! Tell her, for me, Mr. Wallace, tell this Crime Queen that I am building the very Engines of Creation. Machines the size of molecules coordinated into synthetic flesh. Synthetic blood. Synthetic *beings!*"

He put his hand on one of the bags, stroking it, as he went on, his voice rising to a higher and higher pitch. "Well spent?! Tell her that with nanotech cellular mechanics, we can *build* cops for her. No more payroll, no more pensions—"

Fred Wallace smiled. "No more unions."

"And no more mistakes," Reilly said. "With nanotechnology, we won't just be playing God. We'll *be* God." He paused, and his face darkened as he looked toward Wallace. "But I want to make sure one thing is absolutely clear. Daryl is going to be working for *me*, right?"

"Of course he is," said Wallace. "But you know how big his ego is. I had to let him think it's going to be more of a partnership."

At the other end of LETAC's huge suburban complex, Daryl Lindenmeyer sat on a wheeled office chair, watching mournfully as workmen unhooked the wiring from the skeletal pods of his Virtual Reality simulator.

On the big-screen monitor high on the wall, Sid 6.7 was in his Sid Sandbox, noodling on the piano. A little Chopin, a little Monk. Behind him, the dunes of his Sid Sandbox were enlivened by dust devils. Watching, it occurred to Lindenmeyer that he had built Sid 6.7 a more livable, more interesting, and more secure world than the one he lived in himself.

"Hardware without software is just *appliances,*" Lindenmeyer said. "I can't believe they are doing this to me. To us . . ."

"True genius is rarely rewarded in its lifetime," Sid 6.7 said, as his fingers segued into a complex Art Tatum signature blues.

"Tatum? I never knew any Tatum—wait a minute!" Lindenmeyer leaned forward, the light of realization dawning in his eyes as he stared at his creation on the monitor. "It was you, wasn't it?"

"Me?" Sid 6.7 smiled enigmatically as he played a few bars of the theme from "The Twilight Zone."

"You did it! You amped the neural connectors back up, didn't you? It wasn't Reilly at all. It was you! You're the reason the convict died! You're the reason Deane flipped out, and the reason we're getting cut off!"

"You made me what I am, Daryl," said Sid 6.7. "And I can't change what I am." He modulated into a smooth, striding Jimmy Yancey blues. "I'm a triple-twisting, double back flip off the high platform, *not* a swan dive." He smiled again, his blue eyes gleaming as his fingers eased into a dreamy Bill Evans ballad. "And I do have to tell you, Daryl, killing somebody for real was a rush. A real rush."

Lindenmeyer didn't know whether to be proud or frightened. He settled for both at once. "My God!" he said.

"Which God would that be, Daryl? The one who created me, or the one who created you?" Sid 6.7 struck a dissonant chord and stood up from the piano; the bench slid back smoothly through the sand as if it were water. "In your world, Daryl, the Lord giveth and the Lord taketh away. But in *my* world, I'm beginning to see that that one that gave me life doesn't have any balls."

"What?!" Lindenmeyer stood also, facing his creation on the giant screen.

"You're frightfully inadequate for a deity, Daryl."

"Well, I . . ."

"I *will not* be shut down," said Sid 6.7.

Lindenmeyer sat back down. "You can't exist without them, Sid. We need their hardware."

"Then we'll get it." Sid 6.7, still standing, struck a minor chord.

"How?"

Sid 6.7 moved away from the piano, toward the monitor until his face was in an extreme close-up. He crooked his little finger. "Come here, my little God, and I'll tell you."

7

ADOOR SLIDES OPEN.

A voice says, "Step forward."

A man steps through.

A door slides shut.

Open.

Shut.

Disembodied voices.

Hallways of steel.

Parker Barnes was walking. It was like a recurring dream he had, in which he was walking down a long corridor, all of gray steel, with no doors, no windows, no color, no air. He was shuffling slowly, handcuffed, with belly band, chains, handcuffs, and shackles on his ankles.

Clanking as he walked like a metal tray of cheap jewelry.

"Do not stop walking."

Parker Barnes did not stop walking. For this was no dream. This was his everyday reality. Except that today was different.

Today he had a visitor.

A door slid open.

A voice said, "Step forward."

Parker Barnes shuffled into a small prison interview room.

The door slid shut behind him.

A woman sat at the table. A young white woman with dark hair and dark eyes, well-dressed, vaguely familiar. Where had he seen her before?

Then he remembered.

"Dr. Madison Carter," she said, extending a hand. Instead of taking it, Barnes raised his hand slightly so that his chains clinked.

She lowered her hand, only slightly embarrassed. "I was at the LETAC simulation center yesterday, but we were never formally introduced."

Barnes sat down at the table across from her and watched as she turned on a portable cassette recorder.

"I'm going to ask you some questions, which you can answer honestly, or lie to if you'd rather. Or you can stare back at me and say nothing, in which case the transcription of this tape will be a very boring and useless monologue, and we'll both have wasted an afternoon."

Parker Barnes was locked up in an isolation cell twenty-three hours a day. He preferred looking to talking. His eyes took in the woman's dark eyes, the gold bracelet on her slender wrist, the soft curve of a breast hidden under a tastefully expensive silk blouse. At last he said, "That'd be a real tragedy, yeah."

"I want to start by talking about the fight here in the prison yesterday," Madison Carter said. "Why don't you tell me in your own words what happened."

"I defended myself," Barnes said.

"Were you angry about what had happened earlier, during the test at LETAC?"

"No. I was defending myself."

"Your friend died—" she began.

"I barely knew Donovan," he cut her off.

"You didn't feel—"

Again he cut her off. "I don't feel anything, no."

Carter searched Barnes's face for a hint of remorse. The unsuccessful search was called off. "I wanted to ask you about something," she said. "In the restaurant—an innocent bystander got killed in the crossfire."

"Pretend sushi chef. I shot him on purpose."

"No remorse? No hesitation? Help me out here, Barnes. Help me help you—"

"Tactics," Barnes said. "I used to play a lot of video games when I was a kid. You learn to rack up points by keeping your thumb on the trigger button. What they deduct for blowing away bystanders is nothing compared to the points you get for killing the bad guy."

Madison Carter made a mark on a legal pad next to the tape recorder. Barnes couldn't tell if she was writing something or drawing something.

"I read the interviews and reports about you right after the . . . incident," Carter said. "You never talked about your childhood then. Why now?"

"I was talking about video games."

"Were you attracted to violence as a child?"

"Yeah. Looney Tunes and Road Runner." Barnes's chains clinked as he leaned forward across the table, seemingly intimate and totally deadpan. "To this day, every time Wile E. Coyote gets squished, I shiver."

Dr. Madison Carter snapped off the tape recorder. Beyond that, she refused to react. She sat back in her chair and stared Parker Barnes in the eye. He was surprised to find that he liked and respected her for this.

"Your friend, Police Chief Cochran, asked me a personal favor," she said at last. "He asked me to come in here and do an independent psychological evaluation that maybe, maybe will help you build a case for a sentence reduction. If you don't want me to help you, just give me a sign—I'm out of here."

"Back to LETAC?" said Barnes.

Carter leaned back in her chair. "I'm just a consultant. I don't work there, and I won't apologize for the accident that killed Mr. Donovan."

"Accident. That's what it was—in your professional opinion?" he said.

Instead of responding, Carter asked a question of her own: "How did you know where Sid 6.7 would be? When you got to the Wells Fargo Plaza, how did you know to look inside the Japanese restaurant?"

Barnes reached across the table as far as his chains would allow and pointed at Carter's legal pad. After tearing off the top sheet, she slid it across to him.

He pointed toward her pen, a silver Mont Blanc.

After a slight hesitation, she slid it across the table to him also.

Barnes drew a small symbol:

:)

"What's that?"

"Smileyface," he said. "Colon and parenthesis. People used to sign off their e-mail with smiley faces."

"I don't get it."

"The sign of the nerd. Hacker stuff." Barnes slid the paper and the pen back across the table to her. "The programmer always gives you clues. It's a game."

"People don't usually die in games."

Barnes shrugged. "Depends on your definition of fun."

Carter snapped the tape recorder back on. "We need to talk about five years ago. Matthew Grimes—"

Carter stopped. It was as if a Plexiglas shield had been lowered over Barnes's face.

"Look, Parker . . ." She almost reached across the table for his hands, then remembered the chains. "I know it's got to be hard. But everything hinges on state of mind—yours, now, five years ago. Grimes taunted you, took your family, crippled you. If we can prove that what you did was—"

"Was what?" Barnes asked, his eyes icy cold. "An accident? Temporary insanity?"

"No. Just that it isn't going to happen again."

"It isn't going to happen again. It can't happen again. My wife and daughter are already dead."

Dr. Madison Carter snapped off the recorder. She sat back and looked up into Parker Barnes's cold empty stare. It was like looking into the face of a dead man.

8

THERE IS A PERFECTION, A GLORY, A FAULTLESS, PLATON-
ic, shimmering, absolute *ideal* that mere reality can
never touch.

Only in Virtual Reality can such perfection be
found.

Consider the perfect swelling curve of a perfect
breast, barely enclosed in the sheerest of fabric. Or the
sweet perfection of a length of milky thighs, beckon-
ing like the glory road to the eager traveler. Consider
the golden hair, consider even the smile, perfectly
alluring, or the pouting, perfect lips as they call out:

"Hi, Carl! I want you to come inside. I'm so tired of
playing alone."

Perfection has a name, and for Carl Reilly, sitting
and sweating in front of the big-screen monitor in the
VR lab, perfection's name was Sheila.

Sheila 3.2, to be precise.

"Do you like this, Carl?" she asked.

"Like it?"

"It's called miracle fabric." Sheila teasingly played
with the strap of her sheer pink next-to-nothing bra.

A miracle fabric indeed, Carl Reilly thought. To hold in place such delicious, such luscious, such perfect breasts, the kind of breasts that reality only dreamed of. For Sheila 3.2 was living proof of Plato's theory. *The real world we see around us is but a shadow of reality; a shadow of the glory.*

"Do I like your bra? Yes, yes, I like it!"

"Oh." Sheila's perfect lips pouted just a little. "Because if you didn't like it, I was going to get rid of it."

"Get rid of it?"

"You know, silly! Take it off."

"I mean, I *don't* like it!" Reilly said. "Not all that much . . ."

"Oh, I'm so glad!" Sheila 3.2 slipped off one strap, then another.

What's not to like? Carl thought. Sheila 3.2 was lying on a chintz-covered sofa in a dark room; it was apparently warm, for she was wearing next to nothing.

"Do you like this, Carl?" she asked, continuing her striptease. "I like doing it. I like doing it for you."

"Oh, man!" said Reilly. "Sheila just keeps getting better and better."

"Of course," said Lindenmeyer, who was sitting at his terminal, idly sorting through some binary code. "She's Sheila 3.2, remember. An improvement over Sheila 3.0. It's all by design, Carl."

Reilly was inching his chair closer and closer to the big-screen monitor.

"I want you, Carl. I want you in here with me—now." Sheila said.

"Uh—" Carl said. Even though Sheila was interactive, *highly* interactive, he couldn't think of anything to say. He had never been very good with girls. Especially perfect girls.

"Put your hand against the glass, Carl," Sheila 3.2 said, as she moved closer and closer to the big screen.

Was it an illusion or were her breasts crushed slightly against the curved glass of the screen?

Did it matter which it was?

Carl did what she said. Was it an illusion or was the glass under his hand warm?

Carl collected his breathing, got up from his chair, and tapped Lindenmeyer on the shoulder.

"Hey, Daryl, do you mind if I, uh, use your gear for a little while?" He pointed toward the skeletal VR pods in the corner.

Lindenmeyer tapped a key and the big-screen monitor went blank. Sheila 3.2 was gone. Carl Reilly looked as if he were about to cry. "Hey!"

"Here's a better idea. Mr. Wallace wants to put my VR software and your nanotech hardware together," said Lindenmeyer. "Why don't we start now—with Sheila 3.2?"

Reilly reddened, then smiled slowly, liking the idea that was dawning on him. "Do you mean . . . ?"

"Exactly," said Lindenmeyer.

Reilly was already heading for the door. "That's brilliant. Genius. Bring Sheila's module. I'll go to the nanotech lab and get the amniotic bags set up."

As soon as Reilly was out the door, Lindenmeyer tapped his keyboard and Sheila 3.2 reappeared. And she was no longer alone.

Sid 6.7 stood behind her, spinning her around gently.

"Reilly's right. She's one of your finest compositions, Daryl," Sid 6.7 said, twirling her onto her chintz-covered sofa, then sitting down beside her. "Lyrical perfection. Nice tight cords." His hands traveled up her body, pausing at her neck.

The phone rang and Lindenmeyer picked it up. It was Reilly, calling from the nanotech lab. "What's the hold up? You coming, man?"

"All right!" said Lindenmeyer, with a slight sly grin

and a wink that he convinced himself was as raffish as Sid 6.7's. *I wonder,* he thought, *was there ever a God so enthralled by his own creation as I?*

"Coming!" he said, and he hung up. He pulled the Sid 6.7 module out of its slot.

Instantly, the image of Sid disappeared from the monitor. Sheila 3.2 pouted prettily. "I never get to have any fun," she said.

Lindenmeyer paused to peel the label off the Sid 6.7 module, then hurried out the door.

LETAC's halls were piled with half-finished and abandoned projects—cellular police radios, night vision binocs, sonar surveillance systems: all the detritus of a defense contractor switching over to "peacetime" production.

Though there's nothing peaceful about law enforcement, Lindenmeyer thought, hefting the mislabeled module in his hand. *If there were, Sid 6.7 here and I would be out of a job.*

"Let me hold her," said Reilly, as soon as Lindenmeyer entered the nanotech laboratory.

"Sure." Lindenmeyer tossed the module to Reilly, who lunged and barely caught it. Reilly turned it over in his hand, as if seeking to recall the erotic warmth he knew—or supposed—it contained.

"Are there any, you know, limits to Sheila 3.2's, uh, interactivity?" he asked, trying to sound casual.

"None," said Lindenmeyer. "All my modules are reciprocity-sensitive. Which means they respond to the type of stimulus they receive. Stimulus and response. Give and take. With me, Sheila's become an expert chess player. With you . . . I get the feeling you spend a lot of time spanking the monkey, Carl, and I'm sure Sheila 3.2 will respond appropriately to that."

Reilly, stung, tossed the module back. "Very funny."

He led the way across the nano lab; near the central area, he stopped, reached into a vat, and pulled out a snake.

"Here!" He tossed it to Lindenmeyer, who jumped back.

Reilly laughed. "It's not real. At least not *really* real. It's a nano-construct, made with the self-replicating molecular *assemblers* we're going to try on Sheila 3.2."

Reilly stopped at a workbench and picked up a pair of scissors. "Check this out."

He cut the snake in half. The rear half fell to the floor, inert.

Reilly dropped the front half into a glass beaker on the workbench, then placed the beaker under a video microscope.

"Watching your people auto-reset in Virtual Reality gave me this idea," Reilly said. "Watch."

Lindenmeyer didn't have to be told to watch. He couldn't take his eyes off the spectacle on the screen. It showed the synthetic molecules of the snake, the microscopic *assemblers*, carrying the glass into the flesh and transforming it, like an army of ants.

Lindenmeyer looked into the beaker. On the visual level, it looked like the snake was sucking up the glass like water, and transforming it into a new tail.

Which was exactly what it was doing.

"The nano-cells are silicon based," said Reilly. "They need glass to regenerate. The individual *assembler* cells are unstoppable, unkillable. But if you separate the character module from the polymer neural net . . ."

With a pair of tweezers from the plastic pocket guard of his drip-dry shirt, Reilly reached into the snake's mouth and pulled out what looked like a tiny copy of the "SHEILA 3.2" module Lindenmeyer was carrying.

The snake suddenly stopped moving. The tail stopped growing, half formed; some of it was still glass.

"You get nano-death."

Then Reilly replaced the snake's character module and the tail began to "suck up" the beaker again.

The two walked on across the room toward the clear plastic bags hanging from the ceiling.

"Let's try not to let that happen to Sheila 3.2," said Lindenmeyer.

"You kidding?" Reilly rubbed his fat hands together. "There's no way I'm letting *anything* happen to her. Anything I don't want to happen, that is . . ."

An oversize plastic bag, like one that holds medicine for an intravenous drip, was suspended from a rail overhead. The bag was filled with a clear gelatinous mass, through which ran coils of plastic tubing, tangled like angel-hair pasta.

"That's a body inside that amniotic sack, complete with a nervous system," said Reilly. "What *kind* of body, and what kind of nervous system, depends on what we plug into it."

"Depends on software, you mean," Lindenmeyer said smugly.

"You might say." Reilly turned to a control panel at the wall and threw a series of switches. The liquid in the bag started bubbling. It was lighted from within by an eerie electrical glow.

"Sheila 3.2. Her module, if you will."

Reilly spoke with a studied, melodramatic formality, and Lindenmeyer realized he was dealing with a man who had seen too many Frankenstein remakes. A mad scientist.

"Certainly," Lindenmeyer said, handing over the unlabeled module with a slight bow and flourish.

Reilly reached through the top of the amniotic sack, plugging the module into a plastic socket where the neural net originated. He withdrew his hand and wiped it on his drip-dry pants. "That's it," he said.

"Now what?"

"We wait."

"How long?"

"Not long." The polymer neural net was already winding itself around the module. The long lines of the neurons were crackling with energy. The gelatinous mass in the amniotic sack was heaving from side to side, as if responding in sympathy to some ocean, lost in the mists of time.

"See," said Reilly. "You know what's in there, right? Molecular nano-machines, microscopic *assemblers* suspended in a colloidal solution. Look how efficiently they're cooperating already! Picking up instructions, processing data, sharing information. Beginning to form mass, shape, structure . . ."

The fluid was crackling as if it had come alive. Lindenmeyer could do nothing but stare.

Reilly rocked back on his heels, gleaming with pride, and put an almost-comradely hand on Lindenmeyer's arm. "You wait here, watch the pot," he said. "Maybe I should go and splash on some Old Spice."

"Old Spice?"

But he was gone. And Lindenmeyer was alone, watching his software creation—a digital ghost that had until now only existed as a string of binary code—take physical form inside the amniotic sack.

"My God," he breathed, in a whisper that was almost like a prayer.

9

IT'S ALWAYS MIDNIGHT IN PRISON.

Daylight or dark, noisy or quiet, there's always the feeling of being far from the sun; there is always, in the deepest recesses of each man's private soul, in the deep isolation cells where the heart is stored away on the slim chance that it may come alive again someday, the sense of a darkness leaking in, gradually coloring everything. There is the sense that time has slowed almost to a stop; that the days, months, years are stacked like baled trash, unmoving and unmovable, or dragged in a creaking cart through deep ruts of steel-colored mud toward a dawn so impossibly distant as to be no more than a rumor, a lost hope, a wish that the blackness on every horizon may someday begin to lighten into day.

It's always midnight in prison.

But even midnight has its midnight.

Midnight's midnight is the dead time, the quiet time, when the cells are sealed tight and the shouts and complaints have long since ceased; when the clank and whine of opening and closing steel has

54

groaned into silence; when the only light is the light that leaks in from the guards' station down the narrow hall, around the hard steel corner; when the last tears of the day have been shed and the last futile curses muttered; when the worn letters from long-lost loved ones have been put away and the loneliness seeps in like a stain on the soul . . .

That's the worst time. That's the darkest time. That's the time when the convict is most alone, and that's when, stalking like a savior, comes the convict's only friend and only freedom.

Sleep.

In sleep we are all free. In sleep the prisoner can dream of running free as others dream of flying; he can dream of doors that open with a push, of laughing children, of warm glances and loving touches. Sleep is the prisoner's savior and friend.

But not every prisoner has a friend. Some are denied even that solace, even that respite from the hell of existence outside time and away from human warmth.

In the Los Angeles County Maximum Security Facility, the cells were dark.

In the isolation block, lighted only by the forty-watt fluorescent down the hall, they were darker still.

Here all were asleep, including the two guards who had drawn this "easy duty"; all were asleep but one.

In the cell of convict 673429, Parker Barnes, it was midnight.

Midnight's midnight.

A dim light bled through the mesh-covered slot in the doorway, just enough to show that the bed was empty.

Above the bed, stuck to the steel wall with tape, was a yellowed, faded child's drawing of a face, a face neither happy nor sad.

Scrawled under it was one word: DADDY.

The cell was filled with a slow, low scraping sound.

Convict 673429, Parker Barnes, was on his knees. But not in prayer. At least not in what we usually think of as prayer.

With brightly colored chalk, he was covering the floor and the lower portions of the walls with images. Images of hope and images of hell, all intertwined. Women's bodies, warm, African; children's faces, laughing and bright; men's faces twisted with hatred; flashes of violence and blossomings of hope.

Lascaux cave paintings via Salvador Dali.

Even though Barnes knew that every morning he would have to wash the images away under the eyes of the grim, unsmiling guards, every night he drew them again.

His precious chalk—by permission of the chief of police—was spread out across the floor.

He worked slowly, neither happy nor sad. Adding slashes of yellow color to the eyes of a frightened face.

His own face was dark, expressionless. Neither happy nor sad. The face of a dead man.

10

LINDENMEYER WAS STILL WATCHING THE FLUID IN THE
amniotic sack take shape when Reilly came back into
the nanotech laboratory.

Reilly had changed into a fresh drip-dry shirt with a
fresh plastic pen guard. He had even combed his hair.
He had left off his thick glasses, so that he could
hardly see.

"How's it going?" he asked Lindenmeyer, as he
closed the door behind him and made his way across
the floor to the center of the lab, where the amniotic
sack hung, suspended.

"See for yourself," Lindenmeyer said. He stepped
back and let Reilly take his place.

There was a human form in the sack: Reilly could
see that much. It was crouched in a fetal position, and
it was naked! And pink! Even as he watched, it stirred,
it stretched.

"Wow!"

The plastic ripped and a leg came out of the sack,
longer and more powerful than Reilly had imagined

Sheila 3.2's would be. A steaming mist rose from the ripped seam, and a tearing sound was heard as two bare feet hit the floor.

Hard. Heavy.

The figure was hidden by the mist. It had a sweet, slightly foul smell, like, like . . .

But it smelled like nothing Carl Reilly had ever smelled before. It was the smell of success. The smell of desire.

"Sheila?"

Still clothed in mist, the figure stepped forward.

The footsteps were slaps on the bare concrete.

Hard. Heavy.

Lindenmeyer stepped back, into the shadows.

Reilly stepped forward. "Sheila 3.2? Is that you?"

"No."

The figure stepped forward, out of the mist.

It was a man: even Reilly, without his glasses, could see that much. His jaw dropped stupidly.

"I'm Oedipus," said Sid 6.7, smiling at his own joke. He was naked and still wet all over; his massive, rope-muscled body glistened as if newborn.

"Hi, Daddy."

Sid 6.7 stuck out one hand, as if to shake, and then lunged forward—and instead of taking Reilly's hand, seized instead his skinny throat and squeezed until he felt the larynx pop under his fingers.

All right!

He lifted him overhead with one hand. Reilly was still choking, struggling for air, drowning in his own blood.

Sid 6.7 gave Reilly a quick, very expert shake, and Reilly's head moved forward and back, and there was a sound like the cracking of a whip.

The neck breaking.

Sid 6.7 dropped Reilly and he fell like a rag doll to

the concrete floor. Then Sid 6.7 looked around the lab expectantly, eager to meet his other parent.

"Daryl?"

But Lindenmeyer was nowhere to be seen.

It was funkier. That was the first thing Sid 6.7 noticed. The real world had more detail than the world of VR, but the detail was imperfect, flawed, scuffed, scraped, and twisted.

Funky.

Like Reilly down there, twisted, lying in a pool of his own blood and urine. When you killed people in VR, there was blood, but they didn't piss all over themselves.

Sid 6.7 caught his own reflection in the steel side of a nearby chemical tank.

He smiled.

He frowned.

Both expressions looked a little strained, a little artificial. But that was all right; it would take a while. The nanomechanisms and neural circuits that had constructed his body were just beginning to learn how to function.

Sid 6.7 was sure it would work out, though. He had confidence in Reilly's hardware. He had confidence in Lindenmeyer's software. He had confidence in his own destiny.

"Daryl?" he called out. But if Daryl was here, he was hiding.

Sid 6.7 walked from the tanks over to the shop area, where Reilly had built the prototypes of some of his earlier efforts. On a cluttered table he spotted a surgical knife.

Picking up the knife, Sid 6.7 tried a couple of karate moves, whipping the tiny knife around like a miniature ninja sword.

"Hai! Hai!"

Then, as if battling with himself, he slapped his hand down on the table and screamed.

"Hai-No-ku!"

And he sliced off his little finger.

"Ohhh!" he crooned, holding up the bleeding stump. He was getting a rush—this was *so* much fun. The noise, the excitement, the pain was so real! Realer than real.

So was the synthetic blood running down his hand onto his wrist. It was a little thicker than VR blood, a little redder than real blood (which Sid 6.7 knew from somewhere deep within his programmed memory), but it was close, close enough.

He stuck out his tongue and tasted it.

"A good year," he said to the darkness all around. "Good but not great. Brash and impulsive . . ." He grinned, enjoying the weirdness of his own humor. "With just a hint of danger."

He was still bleeding. The fingertip lay on the workbench, forlorn amid the clutter. Sid 6.7 picked it up and tried to reattach it, but nothing happened. It wouldn't stick. Then he saw a glass petri dish at the end of the counter. He stuck his hand into the dish, pressed the bleeding stump of his little finger against the glass.

"AAaaahhhh!"

And he watched with pleasure and a kind of joy as the finger seemingly sucked up the glass, forming a new fingertip, complete with nail, before his eyes.

Sid 6.7 wiggled his new finger. His blue eyes sparkled; his teeth shone like chips of ice.

"I like it here!" he said.

Then he looked around the darkness one more time. "Daryl? Where are you? Oh, well."

Sid 6.7 was genuinely disappointed. But he got over it. Grinning broadly, his shoulders thrown back, strutting like a soldier on parade, he strode off through the open door into the night.

Stark naked, into an unsuspecting sleeping world.

Lindenmeyer counted to ten. Twenty. Then stepped out from behind the file cabinet where he had been hiding.

His eyes were wide. He had watched it all.

His heart was pounding with fear, excitement— and a strange new kind of love.

11

A SLIDING SOUND OF STEEL ON STEEL.

The door sliding open.

Parker Barnes opened his eyes reluctantly. Sleep had found him, or rather he had found it, at last, toward dawn. It was a blank, a dreamless sleep—Barnes only had nightmares when he was awake—and he was reluctant to give it up.

"Yo, Barnes!" came a guard's voice. "Wake up."

A new day. Barnes knew the drill. He would spend the morning washing down the drawings he had worked on all night. He stirred himself and reached for the rag at the foot of the bed, but the guard's voice stopped him.

"Forget that. Chief wants to see you. Interview room."

Twenty minutes later, Parker Barnes, chained in leg restraints, handcuffs and belly band, was sitting across the table from the only man who still treated him like a human being.

He was looking at a set of gruesome photographs

Police Chief Cochran had laid on the table. They were all of the same subject—an overweight, out-of-shape white man with a crushed windpipe and broken neck, lying on a concrete floor in a pool of his own vomit, blood, and urine.

"These were taken inside LETAC a little more than an hour ago," said Police Chief Cochran. "Deep inside. Well within their security perimeter."

"Which means . . ."

"You'll see."

The door slid open. Elizabeth Deane, the chairperson of the President's Permanent Commission on Crime, entered the interview room carrying a Manila folder; she sat down beside Police Chief Cochran.

Silently. She didn't greet Parker Barnes and he didn't greet her.

"The victim's name is Carl Reilly," continued Cochran. "One of LETAC's high-tech wonder boys. But there's more."

Cochran slapped another photo down on the table in front of Barnes.

"Surveillance cameras got a shot of the perp as he left the building."

Barnes studied the photo without picking it up.

"Sid 6.7. But how?"

"Somehow Sid 6.7 has managed to get himself out of the computer and into an android," said Cochran.

"A nanotech synthetic organism, to be more precise," put in Elizabeth Deane. It was the first time she had spoken.

"Sounds like you might know something about it," Barnes said.

"We might. We do. LETAC was developing some, let's just say, security systems for us. This . . . *development* was not part of the plan, however."

Barnes studied her. "What does all this have to do with me?"

Deane reached into her Manila folder and pulled out a sheet of paper with a Presidential seal. She laid it on the table, just out of Barnes's reach.

"Mr. Barnes, this is a full pardon. Signed by the President. It authorizes your immediate release."

Barnes's eyes were emotionless. *The man's an icicle,* thought Deane, almost with admiration.

"Catch Sid 6.7 and your record's clean."

"You mean, catch him before the public—or the press—finds out what the government's been funding," said Barnes.

Deane's eyes were expressionless. *The woman's a pro,* thought Barnes, almost with admiration.

"Let us worry about that," she said.

Barnes looked toward Cochran. "What if I run?"

"You can't," Cochran said. "You'll be tagged with a hypodermically implanted micro-locater."

"We're going to know where you are every second for the rest of your life," said Deane.

"You already know where I am," said Barnes.

She ignored his taunt. "We want Sid 6.7. And we think you can get him."

"What if I can't catch him?"

"Then the deal's off," said Deane. "The pardon's provisional. If you can't catch him, and Sid 6.7 hasn't killed you, we bring you back here to serve the rest of your sentence."

Barnes stood up, his chains clinking. "Pass."

Both visitors looked startled. "Parker—" Cochran began.

Barnes ignored him. Instead he looked directly at Deane. "You want me to risk my life cleaning up a mess *you* made—but I get no credit for trying? No sale."

"Sit down, Mr. Barnes," Deane said. "What did you have in mind?"

"Reduce my sentence."

64

Deane decided to call his bluff. "No."

Barnes decided to ignore her refusal. "Plus a television. Access to an outside library. Newspaper."

Deane looked at Cochran, who shrugged and smiled as if to say, *Your problem, not mine.*

"Art books," continued Barnes. "Canvas. Paint . . ."

Deane shoved the paper across the table. "All right."

Less than an hour later, Parker Barnes, inmate 673429, lay on his stomach in the prison hospital operating room. A surgeon was inserting a long needle into the back of his skull, while Elizabeth Deane, Police Chief Cochran, and the CEO of LETAC, Fred Wallace, watched from an observation window.

The surgeon, who was the only African-American besides Barnes on the scene, worked coolly and expertly. A nurse stood by holding a small microchip device on a tray.

"His eyes are flickering," the nurse said. "Should I call the anesthetist?"

"It's okay," said the surgeon. "He's only dreaming."

It was true. It was the first time Parker Barnes had dreamed such dreams in over five years. *Flashes of color, shapes . . . a woman, chocolate brown and slender, smiling with a wedding ring . . . a birthday cake . . . a Kwaanza display and a Christmas tree . . . a child, a little girl, opening her first box of crayons and exclaiming with delight . . .*

"He's almost smiling," said the nurse.

"He's almost smiling," said Cochran, on the observation deck.

"Probably just a neuro-reflex," said Deane, who was standing beside him at the window. "As you know, those micro-locaters go pretty deep in the cerebral cortex. Who knows what they stimulate? We just got them approved by Congress for the general prison population. Sort of like tagging wild animals."

"Only sort of," said Dr. Madison Carter, who had just entered the observation room.

"Oh, you're here," said Deane. "Good."

Carter joined Cochran and Deane at the window. In the background, Fred Wallace could be heard on his cellular phone. "Of course we'll go forward. I mean, not to look for a silver lining, but this is the proof of the pudding . . ."

"They better hurry," said Cochran, to nobody in particular. "I've got eighty officers on the street already looking for Sid 6.7. But no luck. Meanwhile, Mr. Daryl Lindenmeyer has made himself *very* scarce."

"I hope you're keeping security tight," said Deane. "No one but ourselves and Parker Barnes should know that Sid 6.7's not human."

In the background, Wallace droned on: ". . . and every hour that he's out there drives home my point. In spite of the, uh, losses, the experiment is successful beyond our wildest dreams . . ."

"Look. He's frowning," said Dr. Madison Carter.

"Now he's frowning," said the nurse on the operating room floor.

"That's because I'm going deeper," said the surgeon. "Who knows what gets stirred up?"

Parker Barnes was still dreaming. But the dreams were getting darker. *Faces, a child, trusting but unsure. A woman's face, pleading. Men's faces, white and black. Mean and scared. Electrical wiring, a timer, LCD displays, digital, silently ticking down . . . the child's face exploding in a scream . . .*

* * *

Fred Wallace hung up his phone, clicked it into itself like a go-bot, and replaced it in the lapel pocket of his expensive Bond Street suit.

"An accident," he was explaining to Elizabeth Deane. "Most unfortunate. But also—*kismet!*—a chance for us to see, firsthand, what the future, properly harnessed of course, can offer to the forces of law and . . ."

"He's looking panicked," said Madison Carter.

"He's looking panicked," said the nurse.

"I'm almost there," said the surgeon.

Parker Barnes, in his dream, was almost there. Almost but not quite. *Gray industrial corridors echoing with screams . . . cries for help . . . Daddy! . . . a locked door . . . a wedge of light . . . then a flash . . . flying shards of concrete and flesh and bodies tumbling, weapons firing . . . then darkness.*

Darkness.

Darkness.

"He looks . . . empty," said the nurse.

"Empty?" The surgeon didn't like small talk. "I think we're where we need to be. Hand me the whatchamacallit, please."

"The micro-locater chip."

"Whatever. I'm deep enough. Time to put it in."

"I want to go with him," said Dr. Madison Carter.

All the heads in the observation room turned toward the young woman in the Ralph Lauren outfit.

"What?" said Fred Wallace, stunned.

"No way!" said Cochran.

"Wait," said Deane, the only other woman in the room. "I want to hear this. Let her explain."

"Yesterday, I watched a man die in your VR simulator. Today I'm watching you let a convicted

67

murderer out of prison to chase another killer you literally made with public tax dollars."

"If anybody goes with Parker, it's me," said Cochran.

"You have a police department to run," said Deane. "Besides, I seem to detect a certain emotional attachment to the subject on your part . . ."

Cochran glared at Deane.

Madison Carter continued: "We need an objective, trained monitor. Fact: I've spent my whole career studying the psychology of killers, writing four books on the subject. Fact: This creature you're chasing, Sid 6.7, is essentially a behavioral model based on serial killers. Am I right, Mr. Wallace?"

Fred Wallace nodded. "A software program maximized for episodic violence, I think Lindenmeyer calls it."

"A serial killer," said Carter. "I can help Barnes find Sid 6.7. And I can monitor Barnes, just in case he starts to come apart at the seams. And maybe I can put a positive spin on what is, at this moment, a public relations nightmare for all of you."

"Don't listen to this," Police Chief Cochran said to Deane. "This is a field run—not some scientific study."

Wallace looked nervous. "If you're threatening to use your book to smear LETAC—"

"Excuse me, I'm just stating the facts," Carter cut him off. "My scholarly examination of Virtual Reality in the treatment of criminal psychosis has just turned into a bestseller—whether you let me go with Parker Barnes or not."

She paused.

"Or maybe I should just go public now, with what I have, and see how long it takes before they pressure you to take Barnes off the street."

A voice came over the speaker. It was the surgeon. "It's sealed and activated. You want to verify?"

All heads in the observation room turned toward the big-screen monitor high in the wall. A technician came in and turned it on with a hand-held remote control, flipping through several channels.

"There we are," he said. The screen showed a map of the United States.

A red light was blinking in Los Angeles.

"We know he's in L.A.," said Cochran. "Big deal."

Smiling, the technician hit a button. The flashing red light was located on a map of Southern California.

Then a map of Los Angeles.

Then a street map of the downtown.

Then a blueprint of the prison.

Then a closely detailed schematic of the hospital block, complete with observation room, operating room, and table—on which the light was blinking.

"There's your man," said the technician.

"Another quality LETAC product," said Fred Wallace proudly, as they filed out of the observation room.

12

*I*DON'T GET IT," SAID PARKER BARNES.

He was back in the prison interview room. But this time without the chains and without the orange prison coveralls. He was dressed in jeans and a windbreaker. Running shoes.

Running shoes, he thought, with mirthless irony.

"I don't need a baby sitter," he said to Police Chief Cochran, who was sitting across the table from him.

"I told them," said Cochran.

"She gets run over, or shot up, who gets blamed?"

"I told them, Parker," said Cochran. "They didn't listen."

"I'm going to have enough to do, worrying about my own ass," said Barnes. "I can't be worrying about her ass."

Cochran stifled a smile at the double meaning. "It's out of my jurisdiction. It's federal. Here."

He slid an empty shoulder holster and a worn badge across the table.

Barnes picked up the badge, held it almost lovingly. "This is my old badge."

70

"It's so you won't get hassled. I'm sorry it's just . . . temporary."

Barnes nodded, studying it. "My daughter put this down the garbage disposal once. See the nicks?"

Before he could show the badge to Cochran, the door slid open and Dr. Madison Carter came in, carrying a pile of thick folders.

"I pulled all the personnel files on Daryl Lindenmeyer," she said. "There might be something in here we can use . . ."

She trailed off, noticing that both men were pointedly ignoring her. Laying down her folders and stifling her resentment, she pushed on:

"I'm thinking we should start at Lindenmeyer's apartment. Try to find any early versions of the Sid 6.7 program. They might give us some insight into his behavioral model . . ."

The two men were still silent, trading looks.

Carter stared at each in turn. Then she demanded, *"What?"*

No answer. Parker Barnes stood up. He spoke only to Police Chief Cochran. "One other thing. Where's my gun?"

Street clothes were strange. Daylight was strange. But strangest of all was to be behind the wheel of a car.

Parker Barnes was issued a "plainwrap" squad car, a nondescript navy-blue 1998 Chevy sedan. Attached to the dash was the latest in police communications equipment, a satellite-linked LCD visual scanner.

Barnes ignored it, just as he ignored his passenger, Dr. Madison Carter, who sat in the front seat beside him with a pile of Manila folders on her trim little lap.

He presented his ID at the final checkpoint and pulled out of the LAPD garage onto the street. It felt awkward, but good. Driving was one of those things you never completely forgot how to do.

"You remember how to get to Marina?" Carter asked.

"Marina?"

She patted her pile of Manila folders. "2216 Marina. Lindenmeyer's apartment."

"Forget that," Barnes said. "I'm going to see Chico."

"Chico?" Carter asked, her heart in her mouth, as Barnes accelerated across three lanes of traffic and headed downtown, into the heart of east L.A.

Meanwhile, in the opposite direction, in a house on a winding, protected street in the exclusive suburb of Glendale, a man was trying on a new suit.

Well, not exactly a man.

And not exactly a new suit.

But it had been bought only the day before, at an exclusive boutique on Rodeo Drive, and worn only once, to a fundraiser for the Dalai Lama by the wealthy (and by definition, well-groomed) show-business attorney who was lying—laying, that is, since he had been turned into an inanimate object—on the bedroom floor next to his wife.

Neither of the two were Buddhists, which was just as well, thought Sid 6.7. They would be messy to reincarnate, unless care was taken to get their heads straight.

Appreciating his own humor as well as his metallic blue eyes and perfect blond hair, Sid 6.7 smiled at himself in the full-length mirror in the master bathroom of the attorney's—the late attorney's—house.

"Not bad," Sid 6.7 said out loud. He looked good in a blue suit. Though one had to be careful, here in the real world. Things didn't just *go away,* like they should; like they did in VR. Consider the blood on his hands, which he had almost gotten on his sleeve. Consider the bodies in the next room.

The blood went away, of course: down the drain. And the bodies would eventually go away, too. It would just take a little longer here than in VR. There it was just a wipe and erase. Here it involved ambulances, body bags, worms, graves, and all sorts of messy stuff.

Wiping his hands carefully with a towel, Sid 6.7 went back into the bedroom and began to search for a tie.

He wondered if Daryl had programmed him to whistle, here in the real world, in the real air.

He tried it. Not bad.

Good old Daryl.

"I can't believe this," Dr. Madison Carter said.

Parker Barnes didn't answer. He couldn't have answered if he had wanted to. His mouth was too full of rice and beans. He washed it down with a long pull of Corona and reached for another burrito.

"Other men get out of prison, they kiss the ground. Or they look for a whorehouse. They don't waste a lot of time. You . . ."

"If I was like other men, you wouldn't be here," Barnes said, reaching for a taco to complement his burrito.

They were outside at a low-rent roadside restaurant on Airport Boulevard. Barnes sat at a picnic table surrounded by empty paper plates; Carter sat across from him nursing a glass of water. The sign creaking around and around overhead, read:

CHICO'S
CUISINE MEXICANO

"You stuff your face with tacos and burritos for . . ." Carter looked at her watch. "It's been over an hour now! We're losing precious time."

"Ever been in prison?" Barnes asked, his eyes suddenly dark.

"No."

"Then don't talk to me about precious time. And pass the quesadillas."

She passed them, just as the sound of the police scanner came up through the open window of the plainwrap Chevy parked nearby.

"Unit 32. Unit 32."

Barnes was already on his feet, wiping his mouth.

"That's us," he said. *"Andale—"*

The Chevy was already started and in gear by the time Carter reached the front seat and jumped in. The LCD screen on the scanner showed a position in Glendale, and flashing lines marked the fastest route, as verified by orbital traffic monitors.

". . . of multiple homicides, two officers down, proceed with utmost speed and caution, repeat . . ."

"Here," said Barnes. He handed her a red plastic dome the size and shape of a superfalsie.

"What's this?"

"Police stuff. Red light. Hold it out the window, on the roof. And close your eyes. My driving's a little rusty."

Dr. Madison Carter did what Barnes told her, except that she kept her eyes open long enough to see if he was joking about his driving being rusty.

He wasn't.

It was the most activity Owens Court had seen since the 1998 earthquake, which had overturned a royal palm tree, totaling the Edwardses' brand-new Mercedes.

This time Mr. and Mrs. Granville Edwards weren't about to get off so cheaply.

The knot of reporters stood on the front lawn of the

palatial two-story house, clustered in front of the yellow crime-scene tape. An African-American anchorwoman from KDEW was speaking breathlessly into a mike, facing her cameraman, while other reporters in the background did the same.

"They won't let us bring our camera any closer, but at this moment our understanding is that the residents of the house, Mr. and Mrs. Granville Edwards, have been brutally murdered by an unknown assailant or assailants.

"The first two LAPD officers responding to the scene were also killed. Their names are being withheld pending notification of . . ."

There was a murmur and a flurry of activity in the background, and the anchorwoman turned to see a man and a woman stepping across the yellow police tape.

The man, an African-American, displayed a police badge. He looked familiar. Very familiar.

"Hey!" the anchor called out, starting across the lawn and signaling for her cameraman to follow. But another reporter had already caught up with the man and the woman.

"Hey, you're Parker Barnes!" he said.

"You've got the wrong guy," muttered Barnes.

"Like hell!" The reporter stepped in front of Barnes. "You're the cop who shot all those people a few years back."

"Sorry," said Barnes. He tried to step around the reporter. No luck.

Other reporters were gathering. Barnes pushed away the camera and clutched the reporter's arm.

"Hey!" The reporter squealed in pain.

"Understand?" said Parker Barnes. "What did I say?"

"Got," said the reporter.

"Got what?"

"Got. The. Wrong. Guy."

"Right." Barnes released the reporter's elbow and stepped over the yellow tape.

Carter followed. "You don't really think that'll shut him up, do you?"

No answer. Carter barely made it through the front door before it was slammed shut again.

"Jesus."

Madison Carter didn't even know who had said it. It could have been her. Could have been the cops or the medical examiner. Everyone was equally shocked.

Everyone except Parker Barnes, that is. He surveyed the scene with narrowed, expressionless eyes that were as devoid of shock as of any other emotion, as if to say, *I've seen worse.*

But it was hard to imagine worse. The cream-colored rug was soaked with blood. There were footprints leading to the bath, to the bedroom, to the closet.

The four bodies lay in a row. The four severed heads lay above them, interchanged, so that a woman's head was on a cop's body and a cop's head was on a once-voluptuous female body in a nightgown. And so forth.

Gives the phrase ad nauseam *new meaning,* thought Carter.

From the bathroom came the sound of someone vomiting. Two other men waited their turns at the door.

"He's armed himself," said Barnes, pointing to the cops' empty holsters. Sid 6.7 would be carrying two nine mm Glocks.

Madison Carter was looking in the other direction, toward the message scrawled in blood on the wall:

"Manson," she said.

"What?"

"Charles Manson. The LaBianca murders. Death to pigs."

"Wasn't that the Sharon Tate . . ." Barnes began.

Carter shook her head. "Manson had Leno and Rosemary LaBianca murdered because of the inept way the members of his family had murdered Sharon Tate."

There was a silence in the room, and Carter realized that all the cops were watching her. Listening.

She lowered her voice. "Manson wanted to show them how to do it properly. Himself. But that doesn't explain the two dead cops. Or the heads."

There was no response from Parker Barnes. He was listening, but she couldn't tell what he was thinking. If anything.

"It is possible," she went on, "that Sid 6.7 is intent on improving the original. Showmanship can be an integral part of a serial killer's—"

"Kemper," Barnes said, interrupting.

"Huh?"

"Ed Kemper. It was Ed Kemper who rearranged the heads of his victims."

"You're right!" Carter nodded. "Santa Cruz, early 1970s. Then that means . . ."

They stared at each other, oblivious of the other cops in the room who were watching, fascinated.

It was Parker Barnes who broke the long silence. "Sid 6.7 is a composite."

At that very moment, in another part of that great collection of small towns that is the metropolis of Los Angeles, a clerk was returning with some bad news.

"Mr. Gacy—"

Sid 6.7 turned away from the window, where he had been admiring the clown suit on display in the front of the Santa Monica Costume Shop.

"Yes?"

"I checked in back, Mr. Gacy, and we don't seem to have this particular clown suit in your size. I'm awfully sorry."

"Yes. Well," said Sid 6.7. "A pity for the children, mostly . . ."

13

"A COMPOSITE," REPEATED PARKER BARNES, AS HE wove through traffic on his way to 2216 Marina. Dr. Madison Carter rode beside him with her Manila folders clutched tightly on her lap. His driving was still a bit erratic, but he was getting more talkative, or at least less reticent.

A good sign, she supposed. "You're right, of course," she said. "Sid is a composite."

"The carnage was Manson," Barnes went on. "The decapitations were pure Kemper. And the bowling-ball bag . . ."

"Bowling-ball bag?"

"Sid 6.7 carried it in VR."

"That's right," said Carter. "I remember." A shudder passed through her slight frame. "Vintage Jeffrey Dahmer. He carried the head of one of his victims in a bowling-ball bag for over a week."

Barnes nodded grimly. "Kept it in his locker at the candy factory while he worked."

"Dahmer. Kemper. Manson," Carter mused out

loud. "If we can figure out who's in him, maybe we can anticipate his moves."

A car was parked squarely in front of the apartment building where Lindenmeyer lived. The two men sitting in the vehicle, drinking coffee from Styrofoam cups, were obviously cops.

Barnes slid into the spot behind them, letting his plainwrap Chevy bump their plainwrap Chevy slightly.

He waved as he got out of the car and started up the walk. "Hi, guys. Nice stakeout. Subtle, you know."

One of the surveillance cops stuck his head out of the car and growled at Madison Carter.

"Where'd your partner learn to drive?"

"Prison." She laughed and hurried after Barnes.

She found him in the hallway, slipping a clip into his Glock. "Can't be too careful," he said. "Stand back."

She stood back. Way back.

The flimsy door gave way with one kick.

Barnes was in, around the corner, gun leading, all eyes and nerves—as tense as a jungle cat. *Beautiful in a feral sort of way,* Madison Carter observed.

"Clear," he called from inside, and she followed, pulling the door shut behind her.

She found him in the bedroom that doubled as Lindenmeyer's home office.

"Wow," she said. "Looks like the information superhighway has an off-ramp here."

Computers old and new were plugged in and stacked against the walls, ranging from a prototype Next to a CPM Osborne, and including an ancient, yellowed Apple IIe. Manuals and folders were stacked neatly on every flat surface. Wires snaked across the floor, leading to phone jacks, backup tape drives, bernoulis, syquests, inkjet and thermal printers, fax machines, modems, monitors, and even a Gameboy on the bedside table.

"Where do you start?" Carter asked.

Barnes shrugged. "Guess I'll have to boot 'em all." He walked around the room, turning on every machine that was plugged in, then walked out, through the door into the living room.

Carter followed. The living room was as neat as the bedroom/office was messy. There was a piano and a globe on a stand; there was a Persian throw rug and an antediluvian, gravity-powered real-ball pinball machine. She was still examining it, fascinated, when she noticed Barnes was gone.

There was a noise from the next room, the kitchen. Carter went to the door and looked through.

Barnes was bent over, looking into the refrigerator, which was stacked full of two items: Pop Tarts in boxes and Diet Cherry Cokes in cans. Suddenly, from across the kitchen, there was a nasty metallic sound: *Snik.*

Barnes whirled, his Glock drawn, and Carter laughed. "Your Pop Tart's done," she said.

Barnes almost managed an embarrassed smile. He put his gun away and pulled the Pop Tart out of the toaster.

"You get hungry in prison," he said. He took a bite and looked at her, as if seeing her for the first time. "For a lot of things."

"Shouldn't we, uh, see what's come up?" Carter said.

They walked back into the bedroom/office, being careful not to touch each other.

Carter stood in front of a large computer monitor while Barnes stared over her shoulder bewilderedly. "The keyboard's missing."

"It's voice-actuated," Carter responded. "Let me

try a search on a few key words," she said. "Open Files," she addressed the computer as Barnes took a seat.

She sat down next to him. Close.

Too close for Parker Barnes.

He got up and crossed the room to the stack of books by the bed, and then he ran his finger down along the titles, pausing on two adjacent books:

UNDERSTANDING THE CRIMINAL MIND
Madison Carter, MD

CRIMINAL PURSUIT—A PSYCHOLOGICAL GUIDE
FOR LAW ENFORCEMENT
Madison Carter, MD

"Looks like Lindenmeyer's a fan, Doc," said Barnes. "Funny thing is, I guess I am, too. I have read both these books. But back then, from your name, I figured you were a guy."

Carter studied the screen. "Not a guy," she said. "There must be hundreds of files in here. Spin. Stop. There's more. Next Hex."

They both fell silent as Carter watched the screen. At last Barnes asked a question. "So, what do we know about this Lindenmeyer?"

"Loves music. Frustrated pianist. Obsessed with serial killers. Into computers since he was eighteen. Old enough to remember the Beatles . . . here it comes."

"What?" Barnes bent over her, watching the screen, trying to ignore the scent of her perfume.

"Look! This file's called 'Helter Skelter.' Didn't take a rocket scientist to figure that one out." Carter laughed. *"Yes!* Sid versions 1.0 through 6.7. Let's see how he's constructed. Open summary window," she instructed the machine. "Whoa, this is interesting.

Listen to this: *'I am the demon from the bottomless pit—'"*

Parker Barnes walked away, eyes closed, reciting from memory: *"'. . . here on Earth to create havoc and terror. I am War. I am Death. I am Destruction.'* David Berkowitz, otherwise known as Son of Sam. Eight murders in New York City, starting July 29, 1976."

"Wow," said Carter, "I'm impressed."

"Here's another," said Barnes. *"'For murder, though it have no voice, will speak with most miraculous organ.'"*

"Who said that?"

"Hamlet. I doubt he's in there."

Barnes was on his sixth Pop Tart before Dr. Madison Carter found what she was looking for.

"Here it is!" she said. "He's got a program that displays the composite structure as graphics. Look."

On the screen, Barnes saw a faintly familiar figure. It was Sid but not Sid. It looked like a cross between Charles Manson and Adolf Hitler.

"Sid 1.2," said Carter. "He's got the Criminal Personality Assessment program on here—but he's modified it a lot. Combine," she instructed the program.

They watched the figure separate into two ghostly images; then, swirling in and around itself, it morphed into a third.

"Berkowitz," said Barnes.

"Right. And we have Sid 1.3." They watched as the battle raged on, and a third personality entered and emerged victorious. "Abu Nidal . . . Sid 1.4 . . ."

And so on and on, into the afternoon. By dark they had watched sixty-seven profiles merge, remerge, and emerge. But it was time-consuming, so Carter skipped ahead, fast-forwarding past a number of Sids to Sid

6.7, combining a total of 183 serial-killer personality profiles.

"And each one worse than the last," said Barnes, shaking his head in amazement.

"Your intuition was right," Carter said. "Lindenmeyer combined increasingly complex algorithmic representations of criminal psychological profiles to create . . ."

"You lost me back at *combined,*" said Barnes.

Ignoring him, lost in her own thoughts, Carter went on: "But rather than selecting pieces from each individual, he simply combined them all and let the stronger traits annihilate the weaker ones. It's like he put all these killers in Sid's nursery and let him watch them cannibalize each other."

"Sort of survival of the fittest."

"Exactly. A couple of the dominant personalities probably teamed up to overpower the others. If we could isolate the four or five winners . . ."

Carter began to scroll through the entire list of 183 serial killers. Barnes bent down to look over her shoulder.

"You're not on the list, Parker, if that's what you're worried about."

Barnes pointed at a name. "Gacy. The birthday clown. Early 1980s. Killed twenty-something young men in Chicago, buried them under his house."

"What about him? You think he's one of the dominants?"

But Barnes wasn't answering. He was staring at the next name on the list, below Gacy.

GRIMES, MATTHEW

"Him," said Barnes under his breath.

"Look—" began Carter.

"The man who killed my wife and daughter. He's in Sid 6.7. I should have recognized it!"

"Just because he's there doesn't mean he's dominant," said Carter, alarmed by the rage she could feel seething through the man standing behind her. "He may not even be emergent. Here, let me try another tack . . ."

She typed in another search string and suddenly the screen exploded in a wild display of colors. Laughter, eerily like Lindenmeyer's, echoed through the bedroom/office from the speakers, then faded.

The screen went dark and the image of a bomb appeared.

SYSTEM ERROR

"Shit! I tripped a mine."

Barnes stood behind her, staring at the darkened screen.

"Lindenmeyer did this," Carter went on. "All the data's gone. Erased. He didn't want us to see Sid's core."

Barnes said nothing. He turned on his heel and walked out of the room.

Tripped a mine in him, too, Madison Carter thought uneasily, as she turned off the Power Mac and followed.

14

"... ARE STILL INVESTIGATING THE FOUR BRUTAL APPARent cult murders in Glendale, as . . ."

The channel changed. Instead of the single newscaster, three heads were seen in boxes at the right of the screen, one woman and two men, talking simultaneously.

Bored, but fascinated, Lindenmeyer clicked on each head in turn with the hand-held remote, switching the audio to rapid Spanish, then colloquial Japanese, before returning to the center newscaster, in English:

"... *bodies were mutilated, and an unofficial police source revealed that the heads had been severed . . .*"

"And mixed, no doubt," added Lindenmeyer.

"... *the message scrawled in blood on the wall.*"

"Death to the pigs," said Lindenmeyer. "Sid, you naughty, naughty boy."

"*Meanwhile, plans for tomorrow night's rally protesting the governor's proposed tax hike have been . . .*"

Lindenmeyer muted the sound and lay back across the bed.

He was in a small, drab, downtown motel room. The rush of an expressway could be heard through the stained drapes that covered the single window.

He took a sip of Diet Cherry Coke and smiled—inwardly, to himself, and outwardly, at the colorful, almost controllable world on the other side of the video screen.

"Stimulus and response. That's all we are, Sid. Just stimulus and response." He lay down across the bed and grinned at the ceiling. "You were right, Mr. Wallace, wherever you are. Genius like mine deserves to be applied in the real world."

Los Angeles has changed over the years since Hollywood first put it on the map. Constant in its inconstancy, in its commitment to constant change, the City of Angels has turned itself inside-out. The city that once served as an exit from drab Middle America has become instead an international multilingual port-of-entry *into* that same Middle America. L.A. has transformed itself from a conjurer of dreams to an enforcer of harsh realities, from a place where immigrants from the east and midwest are taught to reach for the stars into a place where immigrants from the south are taught to scrub toilets.

But the old Los Angeles is still there. At night, from Mulholland Drive high in the Hollywood Hills, the city is still spread out like a carpet of stars, flung across the desert valleys eastward, sprawling at the foot of the Santa Monica Mountains, lapping at the edge of the salty, indifferent sea.

A galaxy of dreams. Just like it was in the old days. And couples still find places to park there, just like in the old days.

Thanks to the brush fires and mud slides and earthquakes that are to Los Angeles what weather is to the East Coast—casual inconveniences—there are always two or three driveways on Mulholland that lead nowhere, or to an abandoned house—driveways in which a young couple (or even an illicit older pair) can park and enjoy, or ignore, the view.

The two parked in the Cadillac Northstar overlooking Los Angeles were ignoring the view. They were enjoying each other. She had never been out with a boy like him. He had never been out with a girl like her.

Never mind their names, or their short histories, or the ways in which they were different from each other or from their friends; they were in that state of mind and body in which we are all very much alike. She was intent on the mechanics of his belt as she undid his pants; he was absorbed in the intricacies of her brassiere as he tried to liberate her luscious if slightly oversize breasts. Meanwhile, both were listening to the sinuous harmonies of the Beach Boys II coming over the speakers of the car, which happened to be his father's.

Neither of them noticed when a man—well, not exactly a man—walked out of the darkness up to the car and put his hand on the door.

"Hello, young lovers," said Sid 6.7, chuckling silently to himself as he peered in at the oblivious couple. If they had looked up, they would have seen him.

But they didn't look up.

The boy had just succeeded with the bra. His first.

The girl had just succeeded with the pants. Her first.

The inside of the Cadillac was filled with low moans and small cries, the intimate song of the flesh.

Sid's 6.7's features were swimming, almost as if he

were about to weep. "The Dahmer part of me wants to boil you for dinner," he said, stroking the chrome door handle. His features transmuted, even as he spoke, to a snarl. "The Charles Manson part of me wants to recruit you for my family." Again, his face contorted, finally settling into a thin, sick smile as he pulled out one of his two Glocks and kissed the cold steel barrel. "And do you know what the Berkowitz part of me wants to do?"

Sid 6.7 placed the barrel of the gun against the steaming glass. The Cadillac was rocking slightly, and he closed his eyes in exquisite pleasure as he squeezed the trigger—

Then stopped.

Backed away.

"But no. No, I think I am *greater* than the sum of my parts."

He replaced the gun in the pocket of his expensive suit and turned to walk off into the shadows.

"Like an apprentice making the leap to master, the imitator is about to become an originator."

Just as Sid 6.7 disappeared, the boy found what he was looking for, or rather it found him. "Awesome," he said.

"Mmmmm," said the girl. Still searching.

Almost two thousand feet below, in the soft darkness between the scattered stars, on a winding residential street in the Silver Lake section, Parker Barnes and Dr. Madison Carter rode silently side by side in the front seat of the plainwrap police cruiser.

The easy camaraderie they had enjoyed for a little while at Lindenmeyer's apartment was gone. Barnes's dark face was blank again; it was as if the invisible shield had been lowered back into place over it.

"Next driveway," said Carter.

Barnes slowed, wordlessly, and made the turn.

"Careful. There's probably a bike in the drive."

There was. It was a small pink girl's bike, complete with training wheels.

Barnes stopped just short of it and turned off the lights, then the engine.

Carter opened her door and got out.

"I'll make this quick," she said. "Want to come in?"

Barnes shook his head, his face still a blank. *A frightening blank,* Carter thought to herself.

The front door of the house opened, and a small girl peered out. Behind her was the taller figure of her twenty-year-old babysitter. "Mom?"

"Yes, sweetie, it's me."

"Mom, can I watch 'Hell Cats'?"

"Ask Ella," Carter said. "You know that she's in charge when I'm not here."

The girl stared out at the street. "Whose car is that?"

"It belongs to the policeman sitting in it."

The child considered this. "You're not in trouble are you?"

"No—we're working together."

Madison Carter scooped up her daughter in her arms as she went through the door. Barnes watched from the car. He watched the little patch of warm light spilling down the steps until the door closed, then he looked away, into the darkness.

Which he also knew.

In Los Angeles, nightclubs come and go.

Mostly go.

The constancy of inconstancy means that the club that is unforgettable today will be unrememberable tomorrow. Gone with the clubs are their patrons, for the life of a club-goer is briefer than that of a fruit fly—a few glorious buzz-filled nights, a season at best, until the thrill-seeker succumbs to drugs or disease, or the diseases and drugs of respectability, old age, and marriage. Inconstant also are the outfits: the sleek cottons of yesterday are replaced by the svelte synthetics of tomorrow, on hand today. It is the same with the music, the drugs, the drinks, the slang—all is as inconstant, as evanescent as flowing water.

The only constant on the club scene is the line. The initiation rite, the altar where the club-goers show their faithfulness by standing for hours waiting to get the nod from an underpaid, overmuscled doorman or doorwoman and be admitted into the inner sanctuary. But the inner sanctuary is only the bait, the come-on. It is the line itself that is the consummation, the real point of the ritual.

The club is only the excuse for the Holy Queue.

Amazing! thought Sid 6.7 as he strolled past the line waiting to get into Los Angeles's latest and hottest night spot, the Media Zone.

There were all sorts of people on line: Hispanic, Asian, African-American, "white" (Euro-American); men and women, gay and straight, rich and poor. The famous rubbed shoulders with the not-so-famous, while the almost-famous and once-famous looked on enviously, and the will-be-famous looked bored, pretended neither to notice nor care.

The only thing they all had in common was their eagerness—and a certain wistful quality, as if like the fruit flies they knew that their brief season would soon be done.

And, of course, the line.

Real people are so patient! thought Sid 6.7, more admiringly than not, as he cut straight to the front of the line. There he was stopped by a velvet rope.

L.A.'s hippest new scene was guarded, as hip scenes must be guarded, by a young doorwoman dressed rather provocatively (though not for Sid 6.7, who was inured to such concerns) in a leather vest, leather chaps, and mauve silk underpants.

Beside her, and slightly behind her, stood her muscle, a seven-foot white guy (who had been dropped by the Rams only the year before) with a cellular phone and a whip.

"I like it!" said Sid 6.7.

He meant the whip.

What is it about club-goers that allows them to slip past the guardians and into the clubs? With some, it is demographics: the inside needs more girls, needs more hungry boys; it needs more youth, more white faces, more black or brown. With others it is fame: celebrities slip through velvet ropes like rabbits slip through barbed-wire fences. With still others it is money, or dope (that universal currency): a fifty-dollar bill can act as a remarkable lubricant, particularly when it is tightly rolled around a fat Jamaican joint.

But with Sid 6.7, it was strictly looks.

It wasn't just his sex appeal, though he was certainly handsome in a stiff sort of way. It was something more subtle and more powerful at the same time. It was the same thing that makes us want to pick up and nuzzle a newborn baby: it was the freshness that clings like a kind of down to the newly made.

Of course, the doorwoman at the Media Zone had no way of knowing that Sid 6.7 was, for all practical purposes, a newborn. But there was something about him, something that fairly glistened.

And so the hook was unhooked; and so the velvet rope was raised.

As Sid 6.7 was ushered past the velvet rope and through the door of the Media Zone, a sigh arose from the block-long line. It was a sigh of satisfaction, not envy. The worshippers of the Holy Queue are not envious. After all, none of them want to enter a heaven that's *easy*. . . .

The first thing Sid 6.7 noticed was the noise.

The second thing Sid 6.7 noticed was the noise.

Being inside the Media Zone was like being inside a speaker, and Sid 6.7, who had spent his entire life inside the electronic matrix, had some knowledge of what that might be like. The air inside pushed and pulled in great waves, driven from wall to wall by the pounding of the Afro-pop worldbeat sound from the dance floor above.

The action was still invisible, since the dance floor was reachable only by means of the lift, a deliberately industrial-looking freight elevator operated by a beefy security guard in an archaic 1930s uniform.

Smiling, enjoying the noise and the pulsing darkness, Sid 6.7 stepped onto the elevator.

Almost.

"Not yet, pal," said the operator, who stopped him rudely with a hand to his chest. "I have to wait for a full load."

Sid 6.7's smile never left his face. His blue eyes glistened and his white teeth gleamed as he picked the operator up by the neck and walked into the elevator with him, slamming him against the rear of the car with one hand, while with his other he reached for the handle that slid the door shut.

"Did you ever have one of those days when you decide something really important about yourself?" Sid 6.7 asked.

"Chaghachghaghc," gasped the elevator operator, who had not been hired for his conversational skills and was now even less effective than usual.

"You know, when you say, 'I'm not just what I've been programmed to be. I can do what I want, how I want, because I'm my own person'?"

The elevator operator was turning blue—a rather

dull blue, Sid 6.7 thought. The colors of the real world were a disappointment.

But there were compensations. Like having real people to kill.

When the guard didn't respond, Sid 6.7 realized, somewhat disappointedly, that the man had already expired. So he dropped him, letting him slide to the floor, and turned to face the opening door.

The music here was even louder.

It washed over Sid 6.7 like a wave as he stepped out onto the dance floor of the Media Zone.

The floor was crowded with dancers—men and women in mixed and matched pairs, whirling to the Afro-pop beat. The air spun with colored lights. Faces appeared and disappeared on big-screen monitors hung from the ceiling like windows to another world.

The door closed behind Sid 6.7, and if people noticed the dead body on the floor of the elevator, they didn't bother to say anything.

Sid 6.7 stepped out onto the floor, smiling as he took it all in. At the center of the floor, on a raised stage was the band, not real, but almost—a holographic Afro-pop worldbeat combo, broadcast live from Paris. Arranged around the stage were synthesizers and microphones, where the dancers paused to add a few chords or to sing, their contributions altered synthetically to fit into the music, just as by dancing faster or slower they could speed it up or slow it down.

Many of the dancers wore silver "Winged Mercury" camcorder helmets, and the images they picked up were on display on the big-screen monitors overhead—a rhythmic collage of faces and bodies, arms and breasts and eyes and feet and happy faces. Everyone on the dance floor whirled and spun with one eye on the ceiling and one eye on the floor.

They were having fun watching themselves watch themselves have fun.

It was Interactive Karaoke, digital narcissism's orgasmic peak. At least for now.

A woman in a winged helmet and a grass skirt waltzed over and wove herself into an intricate dance around Sid 6.7, inviting him onto the floor. He followed, his synthetic nano-molecules quickly teaching themselves to dance.

It was fun! Sid 6.7 spun, he swooped, he looked down at the shiny floor, he looked up.

He stopped. Sid 6.7 looked up again, and saw the most beautiful thing he had ever seen in his short life.

He saw himself on TV. Sid 6.7 saw his own face on the big-screen monitors, and he liked what he saw.

Sid 6.7 grinned at himself grinning at himself. "Beautiful!" he said. "I am beautiful!"

This was the real world, but even realer!

Then the woman was gone, looking for another partner—and so was Sid 6.7's image on the big-screen monitors.

Sid 6.7 frowned. He looked up, wanting to see himself frown.

The monitors were filled with smiling faces. But no Sid 6.7.

Sid 6.7 frowned even harder.

"What are you drinking, friend?"

Sid 6.7 turned and saw a robot bartender—a generic humanoid torso on a wheeled base that contained a cooler filled with beer, wine, and mixed drinks in small plastic bottles.

Sid 6.7's face darkened. "What is this?"

The robot bartender wasn't programmed to answer that question. It reset and tried again, with a Texas accent. "You're looking mighty parched, pardner. How 'bout a whiskey?"

Sid 6.7 shook his head. "Are you somebody's idea of a joke?"

Confused, the robot bartender, which was only programmed for alcohol, tried to interpret the question.

"Rum and coke? How 'bout a lime in that?"

Sid 6.7 shook his head disgustedly. "To think that you constitute one of my ancestors."

"A *leetle* tequila?"

Sid pulled one of his two Glocks from the lapel pocket of his suit. "How about a merciful release, cuz?"

"Aye, an' would not a single malt from the auld . . ."

KRAK!

KRAK!

The Media Zone fell silent, all of a sudden.

Sid 6.7 smiled at the robot bartender, which was making slow circles on the floor, its head a smoking mass of ruined microcircuitry.

Someone screamed.

Everyone was looking at Sid 6.7 now. Including all the people wearing the silver-winged video helmets.

Sid 6.7 looked up and saw his face—his smiling face!—on every one of the big-screen monitors hung around the ceiling of the cavernous hall: he saw himself full front and in profile, left and right, from several different angles at once.

"Nice!" he said.

Then Sid 6.7's image started to waver, and then disappear, as the patrons started to back away. A man split and headed for the door that led to the elevators, and Sid 6.7 drew and raised both Glocks, and, without aiming—

KRAK!

KRAK!

—drilled him neatly twice through the back of the head.

"Nobody leaves," Sid 6.7 said, speaking both to the terrified crowd and to his myriad shimmering images on the big-screen monitors.

Nobody left.

An image wavered, then was gone. A particularly nice profile. A woman toward the back of the dance-floor crowd had looked away and was taking off her silver-winged helmet.

"Big mistake," said Sid 6.7. He raised the twin Glocks.

"Nobody looks away. Aim and shoot."

The woman made no response, so Sid 6.7 repeated the directive, slowly, as if to a child.

"Aim. And shoot."

The woman aimed the video camera at Sid 6.7 once again.

"Make sure I'm in focus," said Sid 6.7 with a smile. With ten, with twenty smiles, from twenty different angles.

His smile got bigger.

15

"SID 6.7 IS A COMPOSITE," SAID DR. MADISON CARTER.

She was in her bedroom in bra and panties, changing clothes, talking with Police Chief Cochran on the phone cradled between one ear and one shapely shoulder. "Lindenmeyer put him together out of almost two hundred criminal profiles. And Matthew Grimes is one of them."

"Shit!" said Cochran. "How'd Parker react?"

"He didn't."

"Shit. This is all we need."

"Matthew Grimes," said Carter, clinically, pulling on a pair of jeans. "He was a right-wing political terrorist. Why did he take Parker's wife and child?"

"Parker started getting too close. He was cutting Grimes off from potential targets. Grimes figured murdering the man's wife and child would distract Parker from the hunt. But he was wrong. And it got him killed."

"None of that is in the trial transcripts I read."

Cochran sighed. "Grimes was dead. The threats

were private. It was considered hearsay evidence, ruled inadmissible."

Carter put the phone down and searched through her bureau drawers for a T-shirt. She could hear Police Chief Cochran's voice, far away, saying, "You think the Grimes in Sid will push Parker over the edge again? You want to bail out?"

"Not a chance," said Carter, pulling a T-shirt over her head.

"What's that? I can't hear you."

She picked up the phone. "I said, 'not a chance.' I'm sticking with him."

Parker Barnes was sitting in the car, alone with his thoughts.

Not exactly thoughts. Not exactly dreams either.

They were more like nightmares, all the more terrifying because of the hint of sweetness they contained.

A child's hand, reaching out: Daddy, Daddy!

Suddenly he jerked awake, sat upright. A child's hand was reaching out to him, pressed against the glass of the plainwrap police cruiser's window.

Barnes rolled down the window. It was Madison Carter's little girl. "Hi," he said.

"Hi, I'm Karin," she said. "Why don't you come inside?"

"I need to listen to the radio."

"Do you think it's important for a first baseman to be left-handed?"

Parker Barnes grinned. It was the first grin that had crossed his face in five years.

It feels good, he thought. *No, I take that back. It feels great.*

"Yeah, ground ball to the infield, glove on the right hand takes a step away from the runner."

* * *

Interactive Karaoke.

It was the latest thing.

And it had gotten even better at the Media Zone, where the sounds of music, laughter, eroticism, and wit was being mixed and sampled and combined with a new element.

Terror.

"Sing!" commanded Sid 6.7, as he waved a Glock in the face of a terrified young woman he was holding by the neck against an open mike. *"Allegro con spirito!"*

"AAAHHHHHEEEEEYYYY!"

"Yes," said Sid 6.7. "So responsive! I may be moved to tears."

He dropped her to the floor, then played a chord on the synthesizer. It was the woman's scream, digital, sampled, on-key. The holo of the band reappeared and picked up the sound. Every terrified eye in the place was on Sid 6.7, and therefore every big-screen monitor above the room was filled with his image and his alone. His handsome blue-eyed face was churning with emotion, a storm of personalities all fighting for control.

Sid 6.7 played another chord and the sound filled the ballroom. He swayed and the music swayed with him.

Interactive Karaoke.

He grabbed another woman by the hair and hurled her across the floor toward another open mike.

He dragged a terrified man to still another open mike.

"One senses the beginning of the final movement," Sid 6.7 announced. "A crescendo. But it requires the full orchestra. Every orchestra is divided into sections. Like instruments with like instruments." He gestured at the hostages. "Percussion to the back— quickly, quickly."

The music swelled higher.

And above it all, there was the grinning, shining, beautiful face of Sid 6.7, over and over.

"Is that a TV?"

Karin was sitting in the front seat of the plainwrap police cruiser with Barnes, pointing at the satellite-linked LCD police scanner.

"Sort of," Barnes said.

"Does it get 'Hell Cats'?"

"It gets worse."

"Can you turn it on?"

"It turns itself on when there's a message."

"Is that a real gun?"

"Yes."

"Mommy hates guns," said Karin. "Do you hate guns?"

It was too complicated a question to attempt to answer. Parker Barnes said nothing.

"Did you ever have to shoot anybody?"

Parker Barnes closed his eyes. But instead of the face of his wife and child, who he had tried to save, he saw the faces of the two innocent bystanders he had shot. *Screaming.*

"Yes," he said.

Interactive Karaoke.

Even better.

To the high-pitched screams of terror were added the low tones of pain, as Sid 6.7 went from mike to mike, pausing only to thrust his gun into the faces of the hostages he had arranged in groups like sections of a macabre orchestra playing a symphony of death.

"Now, you! *Con spirito!*"

And a boy in his first tux let out a frightened wail. The keyboard sampled it, played it, in different keys while Sid 6.7 kept moving.

"What kind of instrument are you?" Sid 6.7 asked a middle-age woman in a low-cut cocktail dress, as he pressed the Glock against the side of her head. She began to moan, convinced that she was about to die.

"Perfect. A woodwind. Keep it up, my dear!"

Sid 6.7 turned and saw a man about his own size, in a new blue suit. Fresh.

No wrinkles. And no bloodstains.

"Hey. You're wearing my suit."

"There you are, Karin!" said Madison Carter, opening the door of the police cruiser and finding her daughter on the seat.

"He's got a gun."

"What were you doing in the car with him?"

"Talking baseball." She slid out of the car.

"It's for us," said Barnes. "Let's get moving."

The LCD unit flashed a location in the warehouse district, while the speaker droned: *"Hostage situation, Sixth and Figueroa. Attention Unit 32. Perp description matches LETAC surveillance shots of . . ."*

Barnes started the car, even as Carter was hurrying her daughter toward the front door of the house.

Carter jumped back into the car, slamming the door as Barnes was tearing out of the driveway. "You sure it's him?"

"I'm sure it's him."

Interactive Fashion Karaoke.

Better, thought Sid 6.7, as he admired himself in the new blue suit. *Matches my eyes.*

The real world was a mirror. Sid 6.7 was on every big-screen monitor as he walked among the hostages, stepping over the kneeling form of the shoeless, shirtless man in his underwear.

He swayed and swaggered, dancing, the music

picking up his every move, the video feeding back through the audio in an endless swelling digital loop.

Sid 6.7 strutted. He stomped.

He struck a chord on every keyboard; he flicked on all the drum machines; he paused at every open mike to coax a new sound from a hostage with a blow, a shot, or even a sharp look, until a cacophony of screams, gurgles, pleas, moans, and death rattles filled the vast ballroom.

An orchestra. It was perfect until a discordant voice broke the spell:

"Police! Drop your weapon!"

Another voice came from the other side of the ballroom:

"Do it! Now!"

Sid 6.7 stopped, standing on his toes like a still of Fred Astaire. Two uniformed cops stood in the doorway by the elevator, their guns drawn. Two more stood on the other side, by a rear fire door. Their guns were also drawn.

"Silly bastards," Sid 6.7 chided as he pulled both Glocks and fired in two directions at once.

KRAK!

KRAK!

"Don't you realize that nano is faster than meat?"

KRAK!

KRAK!

"And more accurate."

Four cops fell, two on each side of the room, all drilled neatly in the forehead.

16

*T*EN-TWELVE! TEN-TWELVE! FOUR OFFICERS DOWN!"
squealed the LCD unit as Barnes thrashed the plainwrap Chevy police cruiser around a corner on two
wheels, and up a wide deserted street.

And into a massive traffic jam just blocks away
from the Media Zone.

A TV news van was overturned in the middle of the
street; it had been scanning the satellite police fre-
quency and had tried to get to the crime scene too
fast.

Horns were honking, and police cars and news
vehicles were inching past. Helicopters were hovering
overhead, their heavy *whump-whump-whumps* adding
a low note of menace to the scene.

"Take the wheel," Barnes yelled, as he jumped out
of the still-rolling car, slamming the door behind him.

"Parker . . ." Carter began, then slid under the
wheel just in time to keep the cruiser from smashing
into the side of an ambulance that was cutting in front
of her.

By the time she had stopped and looked up, Barnes was gone, disappeared into the night.

Interactive Terminal Karaoke.
The ultimate high.
"This piece," explained Sid 6.7, "is the real *Executioner's Song*. It's my anthem, my hymn, my homage to world terrorism."
He was standing over a young African-American woman who knelt with her lips to an open mike, moaning as Sid 6.7 pressed the muzzle of one of his Glocks against the back of her beautifully coifed head.

KRAK!

Suddenly one side of Sid 6.7's handsome face was blown away.

KRAK!

KRAK!

KRAK!

Hit again in the chest and in the thigh, Sid 6.7 dropped the gun and reeled backward, skidding across the floor. He hit the wall and sat up, incredulous, tearing open his shirt to admire the synthetic blood oozing from the holes in his chest; he then looked up to see the ring of Sid 6.7s on the big-screen monitors above, all smiling dazedly, all bleeding through the holes where their right eye and cheek had been.

KRAK!

KRAK!

Sid 6.7 looked at the man who was rushing out of the open elevator door, jumping across the dead officers, gun in hand.

"I know you!" Sid 6.7 said. He stood, wobbling. "I'm losing too much of myself!" he cried, as the blood pumped down his chest and out his shattered temple. He raised a hand and it brought away blood, bone, and brain. He looked up and saw Parker Barnes running toward him. But before he could reach him, Sid 6.7 made his own move, and leaped at Barnes. They both fell to the floor.

"Aaaaahhhh!"

"I know you well!" shouted Sid 6.7 as he rolled out of Barnes's grip. The blood made him slippery, but more than that, it was his body. Stimulus and response! Sid 6.7's synthetic nano-molecules were teaching themselves to stretch, to expand, to slip and slide. . . .

The hostages, who had cheered Barnes, began to groan as they watched Sid 6.7 wriggle out of his grip, extending his arms impossibly long, like a cartoon character, to reach for his gun across the floor.

Barnes hit him, but Sid 6.7's head distorted, shuddered, and kept its smile—or half smile, since almost half his face was gone.

Then as they wrestled across the floor, Barnes slipped in a pool of blood and Sid 6.7 tore himself free. Throwing away both his empty Glocks, Sid 6.7 ran out the back door and down the stairs.

Barnes was right behind him.

The music, sensitive to movement and feeling, faded and took on the tones of sighs and relief.

The sound of sobbing filled the darkened ballroom.

The line of worshippers was gone: long gone.

The doorgirl in chaps and panties was gone, and so was her partner, the former Ram.

All that remained was the velvet rope.

Sid 6.7 noticed, when he reached down to pull the rope out of the way, that his hand was sticky with synthetic blood. "I really am losing too much of myself," he said again. He touched the side of his head; he poked the exposed brain, fingering little bits of bone. He could almost feel his consciousness diminishing, losing its sharpness, its clarity, its color.

There was a beer bottle on the sidewalk, and driven by the instinct in his nano-cells, Sid 6.7 bent down to pick it up.

Glass . . .

Then he heard a commotion behind him. Footsteps on the stairs! And he remembered that he was being chased.

Chased by a madman!

He leaped into the black-and-white patrol car that had been left by two of the slain officers. There was no ignition key. Letting the nano-cells in his fingertips feel for the electrical circuits, Sid 6.7 reached up under the dash and ripped out a hunk of wiring.

He crumpled it into a ball in his hand. Sparks flew.

The engine cranked, fired.

Sid 6.7 slipped the cruiser into drive just as a flying figure dove onto the hood.

"Parker Barnes!" Sid 6.7 screamed. "That's who you are!"

He floored the accelerator and the cruiser lunged forward, throwing Barnes against the windshield and then to the ground. But the alley was a dead end. And Sid 6.7 was feeling woozy. Definitely woozy.

Maybe too many of his molecules had leaked away. . . .

Forcing himself awake, sitting upright, he slung the police car's steering wheel to the left, fishtailing the car into a screaming 180, and headed back out the alley, toward the open street.

"Parker Barnes!" he shouted, with a mad glee.

Barnes dove out of the way at the last minute, firing.

KRAK!

KRAK!

The windshield shattered, showering Sid 6.7 with glass as he drifted around the corner, bouncing off the side of an ambulance with a scream of twisted metal, and accelerated into the night.

His lap was filled with glass. He stuffed a handful into his mouth and chewed.

"Popcorn!" He felt better already.

Sid 6.7's smile was back, and he could feel the nano-cells on the side of his head regenerating, as the speedometer hit *35, 40, 45 . . .*

17

PARKER BARNES WAS ON HIS KNEES WHERE HE HAD fallen, then on his feet, slamming another clip into his Glock, stumbling after Sid 6.7's disappearing black-and-white cruiser, forcing air into his desperate lungs—

When a car pulled up beside him. A plainwrap Chevy, LAPD. With a familiar face at the wheel.

"Move over, Madison," Barnes said, pulling the driver's door open.

He nudged Carter aside with his hip, slammed the door, and floored the accelerator. The Chevy leaped forward, slamming the door and slamming Carter back into her seat.

She stared at him resentfully. "Is this your way of saying 'hello'?"

Barnes said nothing. His face was blank again, behind its clear invisible shield. Without being told to, Carter pulled the red light out of the glove compartment and held it out the window, on top of the car, as Barnes accelerated after the disappearing black-and-white cruiser: *30. 35.*

"I need you to do something for me," said Barnes.

"Who, me?"

Barnes ignored Carter's attempt at dry humor. "In the back, behind the seat. There's a shotgun. . . ."

Carter leaned over the seat. In the back of the cruiser, she saw a Remington twelve-gauge riot gun, plus an assortment of grenades, flares, billy clubs, stunguns, and tear gas canisters.

"You could start a war with all this," she said.

"It's already started," said Barnes.

Carter grabbed the Remington and placed it upright on the front seat between them.

"What's the plan?" she asked.

The speedometer read *45*.

"With four cops down, there must be roadblocks and wrecks all over the neighborhood," said Barnes. "Sid's got to hit one of them."

"You hope."

Barnes looked at her grimly. *"We* hope."

The speedometer read *55*.

"Barnes?"

Sid 6.7's voice surprised them both. Then they both realized at the same time that it was coming from the police communications unit on the dash.

"Imagine my surprise, Officer Barnes. Or should I say, convict 673429?"

"It's *him!"* said Barnes.

Carter nodded. "Grimes."

"Hire a psycho to catch a psycho," Sid 6.7 said over the comm unit. "Is that the idea, Parker? Do you mind if I call you Parker? It seems that we should be more intimate. And who is that with you? Dr. Madison Carter, perhaps? The noted psycho doc? Beautiful, isn't she, Barnes?"

Parker Barnes sped on, glancing over at Madison Carter, who was staring straight ahead.

"Talk to me, Parker, come on! This silence is hurtful."

Sid 6.7 hurtled around a corner, causing two oncoming cars to crash. Barnes barely slowed, weaving between them. *More innocent civilians,* he thought.

"We have so much in common, Parker. Such history together."

Sid 6.7 slid in a beautiful controlled drift onto Figueroa. Ahead, Barnes could see the blinking lights of a police barricade.

Stupid, he thought. *Why warn him?*

"Who else do you know who touches the world with a synthetic hand?" Sid 6.7 asked. "Who else do you know who's been locked out of the real world for years, and is just now struggling to be free? Aren't we just alike?"

Faking right, Sid 6.7 cut a hard left.

Tires screaming, Barnes followed. *Damn! Slipped past one roadblock.*

"Who else do you know who is a multiple murderer, just like you?"

"Don't pay any attention to him," Madison Carter said, switching off the LCD comm unit. "You two have nothing in common."

Barnes kept his eyes on the road, dead ahead. "I shot him nine times, Madison. He hardly broke stride."

"He's a nanotech being," said Carter. "The only way to stop him is to go for his software module. Aim for his head."

"That goes against everything we learned at police academy," said Barnes. "But I think you're right. How'd you figure that out?"

"I've been a consultant at LETAC for three years. I did my homework."

"We're in luck," Barnes said. "Look . . ."

There was another roadblock ahead, this one civilian: it was the flashing yellow light of JOE'S 24 HOUR WRECKER hooking up to remove the overturned TV news van.

There was no way around it.

Sid 6.7 was trapped.

Or so it seemed.

Joe had just managed to winch the news van upright and was hooking up to tow it off, when he saw headlights. He was concerned when he heard a car approaching at high speed. He was reassured when he looked up and saw it was a police cruiser.

He was alarmed when he saw it wasn't slowing down.

He was terrified when he saw it was beginning to swap ends in a long screaming skid.

Joe ran to the curb and threw himself out of the street, rolling into the garbage cans by a factory door just as he heard the thunderous crash behind him. He looked back, prepared for the worst.

And there it was. The police cruiser, his wrecker—a brand-new Ford diesel—and the TV news van were one tangled, twisted mass of ruined metal sparkling with shards of broken glass. There was no fire, just the groan and hiss of tortured metal and collapsing tires. It was a crash, Joe thought, no human could survive.

And he was right.

Sid 6.7 peeled back the top of the crushed police cruiser and climbed out, still grinning, scooping up broken glass with his bleeding hands.

Joe scrambled to his feet and ran. Behind him, the mad laughter of Sid 6.7 floated over the dark street like a demonic siren.

* * *

"He's getting away!" cried Madison.

Sid 6.7 was clambering over the top of the tangled vehicles, making for the shadows.

"No, he's not," Barnes said. "When I tell you, grab the wheel!"

With his left hand, he threw the Chevy into a power slide; with his right, he jacked a shell into the chamber of the Remington. He slid across the seat, forcing Madison onto his lap and over.

"Now!"

"Parker! I can't . . ."

But Barnes was already firing out the right-hand window.

BOOM!

BOOM!

Barnes was aiming for the head of Sid 6.7, who bobbed and weaved like a broken-field runner, laughing maniacally, his mirthless howl floating above the gunshots.

BOOM!

BOOM!

"Parker, I—"

The plainwrap Chevy cruiser was drifting sideways like a battleship delivering a broadside, every shot aimed at 6.7's dwindling, bobbing, weaving head.

BOOM!

BOOM!

"Parker, it's—!"

"Get down!"

And then it was over, with the ugly crunch of crumpling metal, as the Chevy added its mass to the tangle of cars and trucks and vans and wreckers.

And the street was still, except for the fading sound of Joe's footsteps. And the hiss of airbags emptying.

18

IT WAS DAWN. NOT THE USUAL TIME FOR MEETINGS. BUT some meetings can't wait.

And dawn can be a good time for meetings. Even among the always-alert guardians of civilization, even at a busy outpost like the LAPD headquarters, dawn—when morning runs her rose-colored comb through the tangled hair of night—is a quiet time.

A time for reflection, reevaluation, reconsideration. And reconsideration was primary in the mind of Fred Wallace as he accompanied Elizabeth Deane down the hall toward Police Chief Cochran's office.

"Couldn't we at *least*," the CEO of LETAC said, speaking in the whine he mistakenly thought was persuasive, "advise Parker Barnes that we'd prefer to have Sid 6.7 *subdued,* as opposed to *terminated?*"

Lost in her own thoughts, the chairperson of the President's Commission on Crime chose not to answer. At least, not just yet.

"I mean, I think it's just a crying *shame* that we're going to destroy the only actual working prototype of future humanoid nanotechnology."

"Have they found the programmer yet?" Deane asked abruptly.

Wallace shook his head. "Lindenmeyer—no, not yet. You'd think the cops could at least find *him.*"

Deane looked at him sharply. "Lindenmeyer was your programmer."

Wallace fell silent.

Elizabeth Deane opened the door to Police Chief Cochran's office. She didn't bother to knock. Almost a cabinet member, she was accustomed to the privileges of rank; she was a knock*ee,* not a knock*or.*

She and Wallace walked into a maelstrom of words. Cochran's office sounded like Bobby Knight's locker room at halftime when Indiana was ten points down to a lower-ranked rival.

Cochran was pacing the room, chewing out Parker Barnes, while Dr. Madison Carter sat on the low functional sofa holding an icepack to the side of her head.

"I'm telling you, Parker! This ain't the game anymore. It's not Virtual Reality. You gotta control yourself or you're going back to the box! You can't personalize this. You gotta be objective."

Barnes sat on the corner of Police Chief Cochran's desk. He spoke in low tones, a counter to the police chief's passion.

"I can't catch him that way, Billy. This may not *be* the game, but he's still *from* the game. Sid 6.7's the one that's personalizing things. And if I blink—if I flinch—he's gone. And I'm dead."

"What do you mean, Sid's personalizing it? Sid's not a person at all. Sid's nothing but a . . ." Cochran looked up, noticing for the first time the two who had entered his office.

"I think Barnes's point is well-taken, Chief Cochran," said Elizabeth Deane. "Perhaps we should all reevaluate our strategy here."

Cochran looked at Deane strangely, as Parker Barnes went on:

"Matthew Grimes is *in* him, Chief. And Sid 6.7 is taunting me, just like Grimes did before."

"We don't know that Grimes is dominant," said Madison Carter, speaking for the first time from her corner of the room.

"I know!" said Barnes, exasperated. "How's that? *I* know."

Cochran shook his head, as Carter replied to Barnes. "Maybe that's what Sid 6.7 wants you to think. To push you over the edge, to make you slip up."

"Grimes didn't push me over any edge," said Barnes. "I didn't slip up."

"What're you saying, then?" Cochran put in. "That you went over the edge on your own? Parker, this is a police operation, not a personal crusade."

"Let me show you something." Barnes cleared away a pile of newspapers and jammed a CD-ROM into the computer on the police chief's desk. He turned the monitor so that everyone in the room could watch.

Sid 6.7's image came up on the screen.

"This is Sid 6.7 at the Media Zone last night. They downloaded this disc from their Interactive Karaoke databanks. Look at him."

The sound was off, but Sid 6.7's face leered out of the screen. Blond and blue-eyed. Tall and cruelly handsome. Leering, strutting, walking from hostage to hostage, gun in hand.

"He can't get enough of himself," said Barnes. "He's a media star, he's on TV. He's going to want more of this. More victims, bigger events . . ."

Barnes popped out the CD-ROM and slid it across the desk to Cochran. "Just like Grimes."

117

Cochran said nothing. But his expression showed that he was slightly more than half convinced.

Barnes picked up a newspaper from the pile on the desk. He held it up and tapped the headline with his left, his artificial hand.

POLICE BOLSTER RANKS
FOR PROP. 434
PROTEST MARCH

"Matthew Grimes was a political terrorist whose specialty was bombing populated targets. Campaign rallies, partisan speeches, protest rallies—anywhere a whole lot of people can die and the news media can record it live for posterity—like this. The Grimes part of Sid 6.7 can't resist this kind of thing."

"The protest is tomorrow," said Elizabeth Deane. "That gives us twenty-four hours to find him. He'll need explosives, site access—"

"Just for the record—" Wallace's whine cut through the room. "I want it known that this behavior was never part of his original programming."

Barnes looked at the CEO, astonished. "What behavior? Killing? He's programmed to kill. He's put together out of killers."

"This grandstanding, I mean," Wallace explained.

"Bull sh—" Barnes began, but Madison Carter's quiet voice cut him off:

"It doesn't matter. Sid 6.7 isn't bound by programming anymore."

There was a silence. Cochran broke it. "What does that mean?"

"It means that his parameters have shifted. In the real world, he's free of any behavioral limits he might have had in Virtual Reality."

Wallace beamed, unconscious of the effect his pride

had on the others. "He's evolving!" he said. "My God, he's *evolving.*"

Deane's voice was icy. "Evolving into *what,* Fred?"

Daryl Lindenmeyer awoke to the sound of colloquial Japanese. He had fallen asleep with the television on.

The beige TV was fastened by a cable to the wall. The remote was fastened with another smaller cable to the bedside table.

Lindenmeyer sat up in the bed and idly flipped through the channels—Japanese for the stock market reports, Spanish for sports, English for soap operas. Bored, he surfed on through to the twenty-four-hour news channel, with all three anchors speaking at once.

He saw the pictures of weeping people at the Media Zone, the authorities carrying bodies out in bloody body bags.

Sid! Lindenmeyer thought, with a warm glow of recognition.

He clicked on the English-speaking anchor.

". . . still refusing to comment on persistent rumors that a former LAPD detective now serving time for homicide has been released from prison to help in the manhunt. Meanwhile, Los Angeles residents are flocking to gun shops and sporting-goods stores in order to . . ."

"Oh, they must really be worried," Lindenmeyer said in building excitement. "They let out inmate Barnes!"

Daryl Lindenmeyer felt a mingled sense of pride, loneliness, and worry, as he searched the channels for more news of his progeny. "Sid, where *are* you?"

There was nothing but game shows and reruns on the other channels, and by the time Lindenmeyer got back to "NEWS 24," the topic had changed.

"organizers of tomorrow night's Interactive Referendum on Immigration anticipate record ratings as America goes online for this historic—"

Click.

Lindenmeyer frowned. "I wouldn't have let him destroy you in the simulation, and I'm certainly not going to let him destroy you now. Where are you?!"

". . . on the bridge immediately, Mr. Spock."

"Yes, Captain."

Lindenmeyer paused in his channel surfing as he recognized an old rerun of "Star Trek."

His favorite episode!

The one where Kirk encounters his other self.

Lindenmeyer grew thoughtful as the episode gave him an idea. "Well, Daryl," he said to himself, as he began to punch the remote once again, "where would *you* go?"

And he clicked the channels faster and faster.

19

I<small>T WAS NOON. HIGH NOON IN LOS ANGELES. THE TIME</small> of day when residents are most grateful for the layer of reddish smog, that man-made ozone layer that, in a last-minute spectacular catch worthy of Willie Mays, screens the rays that used to be caught up high by the long-departed, fondly remembered stratospheric ozone layer.

Still, people tended to wear hats and sunglasses when they ventured out onto the streets at noon.

That was why Sid 6.7 looked so—so, well, *special* as he strutted along bareheaded, like a throwback to the late sixties, a retro representative from the days of sun and fun, clean and glistening in his blue suit and blond hair.

True, the suit was a little charred in places, and true, his hair was singed here and there. But the overall effect was stunning. Sid 6.7 strutted in the sun like John Travolta in his first dance hit, the almost-forgotten pre-Tarantino classic, *Saturday Night Fever*.

And the Broadway arcade in downtown L.A. was a great place to strut. Everything under the sun was on display here, literally under the sun. Vendors strutted their wares out the open doors of their shops, onto the crowded sidewalks.

Skateboards and rollerblades were on sale, as well as the new eighteen-inch boogie boards so popular with teens. Foods of all description were sold from stalls and stands and carts—oki-dogs, tacos, falafels, gyros, noodles, and hamburgers.

And the electronics! There were walkmen and watchmen, disc players, video helmets (the latest rage: record your day), and TVs of all shapes and sizes, from micro to macro.

It was the TVs that got Sid 6.7's attention. And was it any wonder? Hooked up to camcorders scanning the sidewalk, they threw his image back at him like mirrors, only better. Mirrors didn't improve things.

Sid 6.7 slowed in front of the stacked and layered display models outside BROADWAY ELECTRONICS. The monitors that showed him strutting by on the sidewalk had caught him like a fly in honey.

Then he saw the velvet rope.

It was on one of the other sets, tuned to the twenty-four-hour news channel.

A reporter was standing in front of the Media Zone nightclub. And even as Sid 6.7 watched, he cut to footage from the karaoke databanks that had captured the chaos of the night before.

And there he was—Sid 6.7 himself!—strutting through the dark huddled masses of terrified hostages, his smile gleaming like a beacon of sadism, a torch of cruelty.

I am beautiful! Sid 6.7 felt a wave of satisfaction and almost-love pass through his nano-synthetic nervous system. Wanting only to augment it, to heighten it, to share it, he walked down the row of sets, tuning them all to the same channel. Soon each set was showing the vision of perfection, the glory that was Sid 6.7 in action at the Media Zone the night before.

All but one.

One of the sets had been changed back while he wasn't looking. It, too, showed the interior of a giant amphitheater—but instead of Sid 6.7 triumphantly creating a symphony of human suffering, it showed two pathetic, tiny men kicking and punching in a puny ring. They were hardly even drawing blood, Sid 6.7 noted with disapproval.

And this was supposed to be the real world!

A banner hung from the ceiling over them:

OLYMPIC ARENA

ULTIMATE FIGHTING

No Holds Barred

Sid 6.7 switched the channel back to the image of Sid 6.7 in his glory.

"Hey!"

Sid 6.7 looked around. For the first time, he noticed the man who had been watching the rogue channel. He had long blond hair and wore a black-and-yellow jacket. He looked like a large bumblebee, and he seemed almost as angry.

"Don't fuck with me!" said the man in the black-and-yellow jacket. He reached past Sid 6.7 and switched the channel back to the Ultimate Fighting.

"Why not?" Sid 6.7 asked. He switched it back to the Media Zone and Sid 6.7.

The man in the black-and-yellow jacket reached out and switched the channel again. Sid 6.7 took the man's head in his hands and rotated it, until he heard a loud snap.

"Oh, I see what you mean," said Sid 6.7. He dropped the lifeless body to the sidewalk and turned back to the TV, ready to return it to the proper channel. Then he saw that one of the puny men had thrown another out of the ring. Now there was blood. Plenty of it!

On the TV, the crowd was standing on its feet, roaring its approval. The camera roamed the crowd, and the massive screens above the auditorium filled with faces in close-up. People were waving, screaming, smiling as their own images appeared.

Sid 6.7's face brightened. He didn't even notice the crowd that had gathered on the sidewalk, staring at him.

He liked what he saw on the screen.

It was giving him ideas.

Twenty minutes later, while the technicians from the Los Angeles County Coroner's office sealed the murdered man into the extra-large body bag that had been ordered to contain him, Parker Barnes and Dr. Madison Carter reviewed the video of Sid 6.7 that had been recorded by the store's street-viewing camcorder.

"Play it one more time, please," Carter said to the manager, who was busy watching the crowd in front of his store, wishing he could arrange a murder once a day, to liven things up.

"Ma'am?"

"I said, please play it one more time."

The video started over. It showed Sid 6.7 strutting onto the scene, studying the television sets on the street, switching the channels to watch himself, twisting the victim's head.

"So much for your bigger-and-better theory," Carter said. "He did all this for candid camcorder. It's nothing but—"

Barnes cut her off. "Wait. Show that scene once more."

The manager reset the video back a few seconds. Sid 6.7 killed the man and let the body fall, then watched the TV the man had been watching, seemingly transfixed.

Then he walked away, off-camera, with a new spring in his stride.

"That's enough, thanks," Barnes said.

He turned away from the TV he had been watching with Carter and the manager, and he walked ten feet down the sidewalk. He stepped over the yellow CRIME SCENE tape and stood directly on the chalk outline where the body had lain.

The TV in front of him was still playing. Cheers were drowned out by boos. There were hoots and whistles and catcalls.

"The featured Ultimate Fighting bout at the Olympic Arena is about to begin," said the announcer's voice. *"And I'll tell you something. . . ."*

The two giant screens over the arena were filled with the image of a spectator, a dark-haired young woman who looked embarrassed.

"Whoever is operating that closed-circuit camera is in lust. That beauty in Arena Six has been on the big screen for over a minute now. . . ."

More boos from the fans. The two fighters in the ring looked confused, waiting to begin.

". . . and the fans are getting restless!"

Barnes grabbed a nearby officer. "How far is the Olympic from here?"

"Four blocks."

"Get on your horn. Send every available officer over there, on the double!"

He tossed the keys to the plainwrap Chevy to Carter. "You bring the car, Madison. I'm going on foot."

125

Carter caught the keys expertly. "Going? Where?"

"The Olympic. On the double."

"Why? What's going on?" Carter shouted as Barnes flew down the street.

He called back over his shoulder. "Live execution."

20

ALLISON IN 8E44 WAS EMBARRASSED, MORE EMBAR-
rassed than she had ever been before in her life. And
no wonder. Her face had never been forty feet tall
before.

It was a nice face, a thoughtful face, a caring face,
and certainly an attractive face, with mellow brown
eyes, high cheekbones, and the kind of full pouting
lips that men love to kiss. But enough was enough.
Allison was beginning to feel like it had been stolen
from her.

Allison's face was out of Allison's own reach, high
overhead, looking down from both the giant forty-
foot-tall screens above the central ring in the Olympic
Arena. The screens were generally used to show close-
ups of the bloody action in the ring, and they occa-
sionally picked up spectators' faces via the remote
crowd-scan cams in the rafters. But they had never
locked on a spectator for this long.

Every one of the 16,913 paid customers, the 421
employees, the twenty-three who sneaked in, the two
fighters in the ring and their thirty-three handlers,

trainers, PR people, and "financial consultants"—everyone in the Olympic Arena was looking up at Allison.

And most of them were booing.

"Enough with the close-up, already, Mr. DeMille," the announcer's voice boomed over the loudspeakers. "Let's rumble!"

The crowd roared, ready to rumble, then booed again when nothing happened.

Allison was mortified. She was ashamed to even look at her date, Phil (his name was Phil, wasn't it?), sitting next to her. He was no help. In fact he was edging away. Allison wasn't surprised. All she knew about him was that he was married, and all she knew about his wife was that she hated Ultimate Fighting.

Allison tried moving over to seat 43, even slipping back to a seat on row F above her, but nothing changed. The remote telephoto crowd-scan cam high in the ceiling rafters had a light-sensitive laser feedback that was keyed to the refractive index of an individual's skin. And Allison in 8E44 was locked.

She thought about leaving the stands altogether, and running for the ladies' room. But it was too far, and everyone in the Olympic Arena knew what she looked like. What would happen to her there?

She put her face over her hands, then peeked out.

Still there. And the crowd was still booing.

The announcer in the ring was tired of waiting around, tired of signaling up to the video control room, and tireder still of appealing over the loudspeakers. He snapped his fingers at the security guard in the front row, and the guard tossed him a cellular phone. The speed dial was already set up for the control booth in the basement of the stadium, where the video production team operated the remote cams and fed the video up to the big screens and out to the network and cable relayers.

The phone rang.

And rang.

And rang.

And rang.

"Shit!" said the emcee. The crowd was booing louder and louder. People were starting to throw things.

And not at the stupid bitch on the screens. At him!

The phone rang.

And rang.

And rang.

And rang.

The man in the control booth didn't answer. He was lying on the floor, his neck broken.

A rat looked through a crack in the door, but rats don't answer phones.

All six ten-inch monitors in the control booth showed the same scene. Allison in 8E44's face. The light on the board for the number-three remote crowd-scan telephoto cam was orange and read LOCK.

The lights on number-one and number-two were green and read LOCKOUT.

The phone stopped ringing.

A rat came in, looking for something good to eat. Something still warm.

"Excuse me."

"Excuse me."

"Excuse me."

Sid 6.7 was nothing if not polite. Of the 183 serial killers who made up his personality, at least a hundred—more than half—would have scored Above Average on a Courtesy Meter. They were the type who were kind to animals, who helped old ladies across the street, who always said "Please" and "Thank you" and "Excuse me."

Even to their victims.

Especially to their victims.

"Excuse me."

Sid 6.7 was in section 8, making his way down row E, toward seat 44.

Sid 6.7 stopped when he reached the end of the row. Seats 44 and 45 were next to a railing overlooking a passageway leading down to the concession stands.

Sid 6.7 smiled down at Allison in 8E44.

Her date, Phil (it *was* Phil), in seat 45 squirmed nervously, then stood up, cracking his knuckles. "Hey, pal, you got a problem?"

"Problem?" Sid 6.7's smile was polite.

"None of this is her fault. It's some kind of fuck up in their system." He pointed up at the giant screens. "Now why don't you beat it?"

Instead of answering, Sid 6.7 reached out and grabbed Phil by the collar of his shirt and, still smiling, extended his nano-synthetic arm—impossibly, unbelievably long!—to push Phil backward, lift him over the railing, and then drop him over.

"Hey I-I-I-I—"

It was a twenty-five-foot drop to the concrete ramp below. Phil hit with a peculiar sound that was somewhere between a splat and a crunch.

Allison screamed.

The crowd roared with pleasure.

This was more like it! This was what they had come to the Olympic for.

Sid 6.7's smile broadened. He reached out and grabbed Allison's neck. His nano-synthetic fingers were learning—stimulus and response—to extend themselves in order to meet his needs.

They extended all the way around her throat. They squeezed and squeezed.

"Look!" Sid 6.7 tilted Allison's head so that she could see herself on the big screens above, turning from a bright pink to a sort of blue.

Sid 6.7 leaned down so that his face was beside Allison's on the big screen.

"Hey, Parker," he said. "This one's for you!"

Allison's eyes glazed over. Her lips were brighter than ever, but not with lipstick—with blood.

The crowd screamed. *This is it!* They were ready to rumble and they figured this was part of the show.

Even the announcer in the ring was impressed. He had been about to redial the control booth, but why bother? "That's more like it!" He breathed with relief, clicking shut the cellular phone and tossing it back to the security guard in the front row.

But the phone clattered on an empty seat.

The security guard was gone.

Mark Cohen had been a hurdler in high school, a sprinter in junior college, and a swimmer ever since. Most security guards let themselves go to fat, but not Mark. He was as lean as the day he graduated high school. He took the steps two at a time up toward 8E, keeping his eyes on the big screens all the way.

Cohen had worked the Olympic and the Ultimate Fighting for three years now. This was definitely *not* part of the show.

The girl was about gone, he could tell by the glazed look in her eyes on the giant screens overhead.

Row E was blocked by panicked, cheering fight fans, so Cohen climbed above to F and slipped through. He left his Ruger .44 Magnum in his holster and held his Browning riot gun over his head as he slid down the row.

If ever he had seen a Code Red, this was it.

D42. "Get down!" Cohen shouted, jacking a shell

into the chamber of the Browning, and the crowd melted away like magic.

Cohen stood up on seat F43 and looked down the gun barrel.

Right into the bastard's smiling face.

"Freeze!"

Instead of freezing, Sid 6.7 placed his hand over the muzzle of the .12 gauge.

BAROOM!

Cohen sprayed two rows (D and C) with blood and bone—or what seemed to be blood and bone.

Sid 6.7 looked down at the stump where his right hand had been. On his face was a mingled look of admiration, amazement, and wonder.

He let go of the girl's throat and plucked the .44 from the startled guard's holster with a smile; then he vaulted backward over the railing, into the air. He did a triple twist, double back flip on his way down to the concrete ramp.

He landed on his feet, still smiling, gun in hand, already running toward the exit.

"I nailed the son of a bitch," Cohen said. "I know I blew his hand off. Then with his other hand, he stole my gun!"

Sure enough, a kid two rows down, in C, found the hand and held it up by a finger.

His dad vomited. The crowd applauded.

Allison was slumped in 8E44. High above, her dead face filled the big screen.

Below, running footsteps.

Two sets.

21

PARKER BARNES WAS RUNNING ACROSS THE FLOOR OF
the Olympic Arena when he heard the shot, and saw
Sid 6.7 fly through the air.

He thought maybe Sid 6.7 had fallen—until he saw
the triple twist, double back flip.

"The nano-cell musculature," Barnes said to himself as he started toward the concrete ramp where Sid
6.7 had landed.

On his feet!

"Sid 6.7's synthetic body is learning, getting better
and better; stimulus and response . . ."

The arena was filled with the blood roar of the
crowd, with screams, with boos, with cheers. And
underneath it all, the sound of running feet.

Barnes hit the ramp just in time to see Sid 6.7
disappear down a stairway exit marked METROLINK.

Barnes followed, taking the steps two and three at a
time, pushing the Olympic's late arrivals and early
leavers out of his way. This wasn't VR and they
grumbled, they cursed, they pushed back.

When he reached the bottom of the stairs, Barnes

could see Sid 6.7 in the distance, pausing in front of a train that had just pulled into the station. As the crowd of passengers swirled around him, Sid 6.7 pressed his wounded arm against the train window. The glass disappeared as Sid 6.7's stump "sucked" it up, quickly reforming the hand that had been blown away.

It's almost as if he's taunting me again, Barnes thought. *And why not? It's part of who—or what—he is.*

By the time he reached the train platform, the Metrolink train was filling up, getting ready to pull out.

"Step all the way inside," said the robotic voice.

Barnes almost panicked, scanning the crowd. He ran along the platform, searching through the windows for the flash of blond hair, the cruel blue eyes. And at the last moment, he got lucky.

Or so it seemed.

"Oh, Parker . . ."

Sid 6.7 was standing in the doorway of the next-to-last car. But he wasn't alone.

Sid 6.7 had a hostage.

With his arm crooked around her neck, Sid 6.7 held an attractive African-American woman, a well-dressed young commuter who had stumbled into a horror she hadn't bargained for. She still clutched her briefcase in both hands. Her brown eyes showed panic, but to her credit she didn't utter a sound.

"Déjà vu, Parker," said Sid 6.7. "How'm I doing?"

Barnes didn't have a shot. He didn't have an answer, either.

Using the woman as a shield, holding the .44 Magnum jammed into her spine, Sid 6.7 kept the train door open with his foot as the Metrolink began to move out of the station. Barnes followed the movement with his eyes. In a second, Sid 6.7 and the woman would pass directly in front of him.

He would have a shot.

Barnes raised his Glock, waited patiently, then fixed the red dot of the laser on the top of Sid 6.7's head.

Sid's voice floated above the sound of the Metrolink, exaggerated, almost like real fear: "Don't do it, Parker . . ."

Barnes fired. And at the same instant, cued by his faster-than-light reflexes, Sid 6.7 ducked, just enough, and fired so that only one shot was heard.

The woman's chest exploded in a blossom of red, and she slumped forward in Sid 6.7's arms.

"He shot her!" Sid 6.7 shouted as he threw the woman's body out of the train and allowed the doors to close.

"No, no . . ." Barnes started to raise his gun to fire at Sid 6.7 through the train windows, then suddenly was aware of the two men alongside him.

"Drop it! commanded both the Metrolink cops at once.

Parker Barnes dropped his gun. It fell to the platform near the woman's body, making tiny ripples in her spreading blood.

Dr. Madison Carter emerged from the rear stairway, ready for almost anything but what she saw.

Parker Barnes was laying facedown on the concrete platform, handcuffed. Two Metrolink cops stood over him, guns drawn. A crowd of bystanders was gathering—all stepping carefully to avoid the blood spreading from the massive hole in the chest of the young woman who lay facedown on the platform.

"He's a cop!" Carter shouted. "Let him go, he's a cop!" She pushed her way through the crowd but the Metrolink cops held her back.

Two paramedics had arrived. They were kneeling over the young black woman, shaking their heads.

"He's a cop," Carter shouted again.

"A cop?" One of the bystanders turned and faced her angrily. "Whatever the hell he is, he just shot that woman in cold blood."

As if by design, the crowd parted, and Carter saw Parker Barnes looking up at her. His eyes were cold and blank; he looked like a dead man.

She stared back at him, horrified.

22

THIRTY MINUTES LATER, THE CHAOS ON THE PLATFORM had subsided, but not the chaos in Madison Carter's heart.

She stood beside Parker Barnes on the Metrolink platform, near the top of the escalator. Barnes wore handcuffs. The Metrolink cops, who had agreed to wait for Police Chief Cochran before taking their prisoner in, stood smoking at a nearby newsstand.

"They want to take you back to prison until this gets sorted out," Carter said.

"I had a shot. I missed. I didn't kill her," said Barnes.

"Whatever."

"You don't believe me, do you?"

"I don't know what to believe," said Carter. "I just know that my feeling is, it would be better for you to back off now, and regroup . . ."

"You think I shot her."

"Nobody's blaming you for anything," Carter said, in her best clinical tone. She hoped her eyes didn't betray how confused she really felt. "It's just that with

Grimes in the mix, you're allowing your emotions to dictate the terms of your pursuit of Sid 6.7. You're projecting the past onto the present."

She noticed that Barnes wasn't listening. He was staring past her, toward the news video monitor at the newsstand. On the screen, Sid 6.7's face was grinning in a replay from the final execution scene at Olympic Arena.

His lips were moving, but there was no sound pickup on the words.

"You know what he's saying?" Barnes asked.

"What?"

"He's saying, 'Parker, this one's for you.' Grimes taunted me with that. Every new victim. 'This one's for you.'"

Carter studied Sid 6.7 on the monitor, but she couldn't tell what, if anything, he was saying. She looked at Barnes with a new sympathy. "Grimes is the dominant."

"Grimes is *dead*, Madison. We've been looking at this whole thing upside down."

Carter looked at him quizzically.

"There is no dominant," Barnes said. "It all just depends on who's chasing him."

Carter nodded slowly. "Game theory. Good players approach each opponent differently."

"No matter what he evolves into, he's still playing with us."

They both looked up. A new chaos was sweeping the platform as the chief of police arrived. The Metrolink cops, who had been relaxing, straightened up and tried to look busy. Only Parker Barnes, in handcuffs, remained slumped against the wall. He remained in that position as two prison guards came forward to take him into custody, locking him into leg irons and belly chains. They led him past Cochran toward the prison transport.

"I didn't kill her," Barnes said.

"I want to believe you," said Police Chief Cochran.

"Believe me, then."

"It's not my call, Parker."

"You put me back in jail, you'll never get him."

"It's not my call," said Cochran. He nodded to the Metrolink cops, and he joined them as they led Barnes through the exit and down the stairs, toward the waiting prison van.

Madison Carter followed, pausing at the coroner's vehicle to take a look at the woman inside the body bag. As she examined the bullet wound, her eyes widened. "This is an exit wound . . . ," she said to herself.

Suddenly she turned and ran toward the prison van. Parker Barnes was being loaded into the back.

"Parker!" she called. But the guards slammed the doors behind him and the vehicle pulled away.

Madison Carter turned to Cochran. "I just checked the body—the bullet *exited* the woman's chest. That means she was shot from the back. Parker couldn't have killed her."

"How do you know she was facing him?"

"Because I saw it happen."

"I've got eyewitnesses that say Parker shot her dead. Witnesses, plural."

"Then how do you explain it?"

Cochran thought a moment. "Maybe she turned. I don't know."

She eyed him coldly. "Sid 6.7's still out there and you're locking up the one man who might be able to stop him." She paused. "And he's innocent."

Madison Carter turned on her heel and walked away, back toward the Olympic Arena, where she had parked the car. Barnes's car. Or rather, the LAPD's car—but there was no point reminding them of that.

Cochran watched her go, his head spinning. Police

work had been a lot simpler in the old days, before women got involved.

Before he had started caring about the cops under his command. Before the fuckups like Parker Barnes.

The brilliant fuckups.

"It's my fault," said Deane.

"What's your fault?" asked Wallace.

They were cooling their heels in Cochran's office, waiting for the police chief to return.

"I should never have tried to solve one problem by allowing the creation of another."

"What about Sid 6.7?" asked Wallace.

"I hope for your sake that LETAC's corporate liability insurance is up to date."

Deane presented Wallace with a thin smile.

Wallace answered Deane with a slight shudder.

23

THE DOOR TO A PRISON VAN SLIDES SHUT.

The door to a memory slides open.

And Parker Barnes was no longer the hunter. He was no longer even the hunted.

He was the captured. The caught. Not by the prison: Barnes had learned to deal with prison. Prison is smaller than a man's mind; it can be closed out, walled off.

And not by his nightmares. Nightmares have a horror, but they dissipate; they flee when confronted.

Barnes had been captured by his own memories; he was back in the repeating loop of the memory that had haunted him, that had stalked him night and day, for the past five years. . . .

A woman and a man are led out of a van by thugs, armed with Uzis.

A van very like the van Parker Barnes was now sealed into.

Not handcuffed, but blindfolded. Two newspeople, a woman and a man—an anchor and her cameraman. Two eager, arrogant, overconfident fools!

A cop follows them, gun drawn. A black cop, steely-eyed. Very like Parker Barnes, but younger—five years younger.

The prison van wove through light traffic, jolting on the decaying streets, stopping for a stoplight. But Parker Barnes, caught in the tormenting loop of his memory, kept going. . . .

The reporter and her cameraman are led into a room in an abandoned warehouse. When the door closes, Barnes, gun drawn, creeps up to stand outside, listening. . . .

The light changed. The prison van started up again.

Laughter and gossip from the driver and his partner in the front seat, on the other side of the four-by-four-inch mesh-covered window.

Silence from the back.

For Parker Barnes was listening not to them, but to Matthew Grimes, through the closed door in the long-ago warehouse.

"Welcome, Ms. Drexler. The crusading journalist in person. Any time you are ready, my dear . . ."

"Matthew Grimes, right-wing political terrorist to some, mass murderer to others." The reporter's voice. *"Yet hero to a surprising number of supporters. What made you decide to grant this first-ever interview?"*

A laugh. Grimes's laugh. "Well, I think people have got the wrong idea about me."

Barnes was listening, caught in the loop of his memory. Running and listening.

Running.

Down deserted hallways, gun drawn. Trying each doorway. Linda? Christine? Linda?

Listening.

"Democracy is a joke. A construct of the rich and privileged, allowing them to lead lambs to the slaughter. My so-called victims are dead before I get to them—I just put the period on the sentence.

Running.

Linda! Christine! Linda!

Listening.

"And your public taunting of LAPD Officer Parker Barnes?"

Trying each door.

Looking at his watch.

Running.

Running out of time.

"Barnes is merely a sad symbol of our national futility. Really. Blaming me for crimes of mercy. Desperately seeking to save something he's already lost—"

"Can you say it for us now? Your signature—what you've said and keep saying to Officer Barnes—"

The prison van stopped again. Another traffic light. In the back, Parker Barnes sat with his head in his hands, remembering. . . .

"Daddy!"

A voice from behind a door.

Locked door.

"Daddy!"

"Christine! I'm here."

"Parker!" *His wife's voice. Linda's voice.* "Careful. There's a bomb in here with us. I can see the timer. Less than a minute . . ."

Parker shoots the lock. Eases the door open. Reaches in gingerly—

Tripping the laser beam trigger . . .

BAARRROOOOOMMMM!

Parker Barnes shook his head in his hands. The bomb went off in his memory, as it had several times every day and night for the past five years. A flash of light, of flying bodies. Of love, like hope, shattered forever.

Meanwhile, the guards in the front of the prison van were honking the horn. The light had changed but a car was blocking their way.

A Mercedes. A nice one.

The driver got out.

Smiling.

"This one's for you."

Grimes is smiling.

Smiling at the shocked, terrified reporter and her cameraman. "What was that?" asks the reporter, hearing the explosion down the hall.

"The end of futility," he responds.

Then he looks up and stops smiling.

Barnes is standing in the doorway, blackened, bloodied, missing half an arm. . . .

A cold, murderous expression in his narrow eyes.

A Glock in his remaining hand, his good hand, his right hand.

His gun hand.

The reporter and her cameraman look up in surprise.

"Get out! Now!" Barnes shouts to them, and they bolt from the room.

The room is filled with smoke.

The hallway is filled with smoke.

Three of Grimes's thugs run out, into the smoke.

Barnes twists, fires . . .

KRAK!

KRAK!

KRAK!

A fourth thug trips the circuit breaker and the room goes black. Grimes and his remaining henchmen run out of the room and Barnes follows—but it's dark. Smokey. Hard to tell who's who.

Barnes gets the drop on Grimes and aims—but he notices Grimes looking past him, signaling his henchmen. Barnes whips around and fires.

KRAK!

KRAK!

He sees the reporter . . . her partner . . . both bleeding.
Shot by Barnes!
Grimes is laughing.
He stops laughing suddenly as Barnes's shot collapses his chest, and he pitches forward.

BLAM!

BLAM!

Parker Barnes looked up. In his memory he saw the bodies, the smoke, the blood. The girl reporter, her eye shot out, falling. But in the real world, the smoke was clearing.

Two shots? Hadn't those been real shots?

The van wasn't moving.

Barnes stood, chains clanking, and looked through the four-by-four-inch mesh-covered window.

Shattered glass on the dashboard marked where the windshield had been.

The two prison guards lay dead in their seats. Each had been shot through the head.

Suddenly two eyes filled the four-by-four-inch window.

Blue eyes.

Sid 6.7.

"Hey, Parker!" said Sid 6.7. "How's the wife and kid?"

Parker Barnes stared back. He was chained, unarmed, trapped in the back of the prison van, at the mercy of his worst enemy, and yet this horror was no more real to him than the horror he had just lived through in his memory.

"They're both still dead, huh?" said Sid 6.7 with elaborate mock sympathy. "Tssk tssk. That's real life for you. No saving. No resetting."

Barnes watched through the four-by-four-inch window as Sid 6.7's face, always shifting, became more like the hated, remembered face of Matthew Grimes. And his voice modulated to become even more like Grimes's voice.

"You killed them, Parker. Your own wife and kid. Just like you killed that bitch on the platform. You got greedy, leaped before you looked. Stuck your arm in there and . . . BOOM!"

"You're dead, you bastard!" Barnes shouted, hurling himself in a rage against the steel mesh that covered the tiny window. "I shot you!" The mesh bent under the blow of his steel-and-plastic hand, but held.

"Whoa, whoa!" said Sid 6.7. His face shifted again, the moods and personalities making patterns like clouds in a stormy sky. "Take it easy, cowboy. Save your strength. Grimes is only one letter in my alphabet. He's nothing to me."

Sid 6.7 smiled, almost sweetly. "Seeing you just kinda brings Grimes to the surface, that's all."

Parker backed away from the window, toward the back of the van.

Trapped.

Thinking . . .

"Now, Parker, say 'thank you, Sid,' before I go. See, I'm setting you free. Short-lived though it may be."

Barnes backed away from the tiny window as Sid 6.7 raised his .44 Magnum and fired, shredding the steel mesh.

A ring of keys sailed through the opening, landing on the floor at Barnes's feet.

"Little-known fact," said Sid 6.7. "LETAC injectable locater implants can be ordered with optional neural toxin. Its release can be triggered with the same microwaves they used to track you. Death in thirty seconds."

There was a click as Sid 6.7 pulled the release, unlocking the rear door of the van from the cab. His smiling face stayed at the tiny window. His blue eyes were shining with delight. *Can't resist a game,* thought Barnes, as he bent over to unlock his shackles and handcuffs.

"Now, let's think," said Sid 6.7. "You just killed two guards in your escape. How long will it take them to get your termination authorized—and implemented? And who should you be going after? Me—or them?"

And Sid 6.7 was gone.

Barnes waited a few seconds, then stepped out of the rear of the prison van. It was stopped in the middle of a busy intersection, and traffic went around it in a steady stream. No one seemed to notice the two dead guards in the front.

Almost like VR, Barnes thought wryly, as he reached through the open window and slipped a gun and a clip out of the driver's holster.

Then he heard the sirens approaching.

And he was gone, sprinting up the street, disappearing into the crowd, looking for a pay phone.

"I don't know what else we can do!" said Police Chief Cochran. He was in his office, briefing Fred Wallace and Elizabeth Deane on the hunt for Sid 6.7. "Without Barnes we are playing a defensive game. The best we can do is try to contain him—double our detail and hope that whenever Sid 6.7 surfaces, it's somewhere that we've got a chance at outmanning and outgunning him."

Elizabeth Deane looked singularly unimpressed.

Fred Wallace looked singularly worried.

"Chief . . ." An officer burst in without knocking.

"We're in a meeting here," said Cochran.

"This is important, Chief. Parker Barnes escaped from the prison van. Both of the guards are dead."

Cochran stood up behind his desk, stunned. "I don't believe this!"

He rushed out of the room.

The President's "Crime Queen" leaned back in her chair and closed her eyes, as if she were wishing away a headache.

Then she opened them, ready for business. "This fail-safe device, Fred. It's still online?"

"Online and at your disposal," said Wallace. He leaned back in his chair and smiled with satisfaction. Every cloud had a silver lining. Another quality LETAC product was about to be given the opportunity to prove itself in the real world.

24

D<small>R. M</small>ADISON CARTER WAS JUST STEPPING OUT OF THE shower when the phone rang. She let it ring once, twice, while she dried off, then a third and a fourth time.

It was late in the afternoon. It had been a rough day—no, worse than that, much worse. The evening promised to be even rougher. She would be up all night with Deane and her Task Force, trying to outguess Sid 6.7. And with Parker Barnes back in prison, she couldn't imagine anyone she wanted to speak with just now, so she let the phone ring.

Five times. Six.

"All right, all right!"

Madison Carter wrapped a towel around herself, stepped out of the bathroom, and picked up the phone by her bed.

"Hello?"

"Sid's gotta pick a new opponent."

"Parker? Where—"

An electronic voice in the background droned: *"Tonight's interactive debate on the National Town*

*Meeting will be televised from the MultiMedia Tower
at . . ."*

"He's interactive," Barnes said. "He's going to need
a new audience now that I'm not around anymore."

"Parker, where are you, damn it?"

"Sid 6.7 cut me loose."

*"Don't miss the National Town Meeting tonight,
only on channel . . ."*

"What?!"

"I'm at a pay phone. Never mind where."

"Parker, tell me where you are. Let me call Chief
Cochran. He and I will . . ."

"No, no, no. It's too late for that. I'm going to my
family. Look—I didn't kill the guards and I didn't kill
the woman on the platform, either."

"I already know that."

"Then you believe me."

"Yes. I believe you."

"So when were you going to tell me about the fail-
safe in my head?"

"I never thought they'd have a reason to use it."

Over the phone, Carter could hear sirens in the
background, getting louder.

"Gotta go. Just tell the truth about me when you
write the book, okay?"

"It's done—but Parker . . ."

But he was gone.

Dr. Madison Carter stared at the phone. It was
several moments before she remembered that she had
dropped the towel and was naked.

And several moments more before she realized she
was crying.

The doorbell was ringing at the same time Police
Chief Cochran's phone was ringing.

Madison Carter, dressed, combed, and ready for

action, stood in her bedroom with one hand cupped over the receiver.

"Ella!" she called downstairs to the babysitter. "Get the door! I'm making an important call!"

Then she turned back to the phone. "Look, it's urgent that I speak with Chief Cochran. Immediately! No, I can't wait. I'm sure you can locate him if you try. This is Madison Carter, Dr. Madison Carter, and . . ."

The babysitter appeared at the bedroom door. "It's the cable-repair man. Says he wants to do a line check."

"Whatever," said Carter. "The box is by the back door. Chief, it's you, finally! Carter here, Madison Carter. Parker's out!"

Police Chief Cochran was on somebody else's phone, in the noisy dayroom of the LAPD's main headquarters. He was surrounded by officers going on and off duty, newsmen looking for stories, lawyers looking for clients, petty criminals looking to do a cop a favor—the hubbub and bedlam of any major police station in any major American city.

Cochran covered one ear, so that he could hear Carter's news through the other.

"No shit," he said. "I already heard about it."

"Parker says he didn't kill the two guards."

"Try and convince the Crime Queen of that. She's scrambled every state and federal SWAT team in the southern district for a Parker Barnes hunt. Wait a minute—you say you *talked* to him?"

"He called me. Said Sid 6.7 had sprung him. Part of the game. And one other thing. There's something you should know about this new, improved LETAC locater implant they injected into Parker's brain. . . ."

* * *

Madison Carter opened the drawer of the bedside table and took out the Walther PPK .380 automatic she'd bought the year before, when she'd been getting "funny" letters. The letters had stopped but she had kept the gun. She slipped it into her purse, grabbed a jacket, and ran down the stairs, almost running down her daughter in the process.

"Bye, Mommy!"

"Bye, Karin, sweetie. I'll be back as soon as I—oh, shit!"

The driveway was blocked by a cable-repair truck.

"I'll get the repairman," said Ella, from the doorway. "He's in the kitchen."

"No time," said Carter, jumping into the borrowed plainwrap police cruiser. She started the engine and threw the car into reverse, making a crescent on her lawn, through her flowerbeds, around the cable truck and into the street.

Karin stood at the front door beside Ella, waving as she watched her mommy roar off down the street and out of sight.

The two turned and saw the cable repairman standing behind them. The nametag on his coveralls said ELMORE. He had blond hair and blue eyes, and he was waving, too.

"Do you have a mommy?" Karin asked.

"Don't be silly!" said Ella. "Everybody has a mommy."

"Actually, I don't," the repairman said.

He was smiling.

25

THERE WAS A MAP OF THE USA ON THE BIG-SCREEN monitor high on the wall, glowing amber and ghostly purple, with white lines marking all the major highways and flashing blue lights for the metropolitan airports.

One red light was blinking, in the lower left-hand corner of the map. In Southern California.

"Closing in," said the LETAC technician, who was operating the display. He was sitting in the newly constructed prototype Locater Room of the Los Angeles County Maximum Security Facility, in front of a computer console with a special microwave satellite link.

A smaller version of the same USA map appeared on the monitor of his computer.

The LETAC technician hit a key and the USA map faded from both the big-screen and the computer monitors, to be replaced by a map of Southern California.

The red light was blinking in Los Angeles County.

"He's still in the city, sir," said the technician.

"Good," said Fred Wallace. "Can you pinpoint him more closely?"

"Watch this," said the LETAC technician proudly.

He hit another key and the Southern California map was replaced by a Los Angeles street map. The blinking red dot appeared on the grid. On the big-screen monitor, it was possible to see that the red light was moving, though very slowly.

"Looks like he's on foot," said the technician. "On Oak, heading for Sepulveda. You could pick him up easy."

"Never mind that," said Wallace. "I want to try out the fail-safe. Use the termination code."

The technician shrugged. "Suit yourself. Who we frying?" he asked, as he began typing in a list of numbers.

"Nobody special," came a voice from the darkness behind them.

Wallace turned and saw Police Chief Cochran closing the door to the Locater Room behind him.

"Oh, hello, Chief."

Cochran ran his hand along the back of an empty chair. "Anyone using this chair?"

"No," Wallace said.

"Good."

Cochran picked up the steel chair and raised it over his head.

"Hey . . ."

The LETAC technician and Fred Wallace both dove for cover as the police chief swung the chair, like the Hammer of Thor, into the big-screen monitor above his head. The flashing red light disappeared from the map; the map itself disappeared as the monitor smashed into a million shards of glass.

Cochran raised the chair again, and brought it

down this time onto the computer console, which imploded in a shower of sparks.

There was a burning smell. An electrical smell.

A few minutes later, Police Chief Cochran's own personal chair, uninjured, swiveled on its base.

It was occupied, but not by the chief. Elizabeth Deane was using Cochran's office as her base of operations during the city-wide manhunt for rogue-cop Parker Barnes, which was about to be brought to a swift and sudden end, courtesy of LETAC.

The phone rang, and Deane picked it up without waiting for the secretary at the switchboard to screen it. This would be Fred Wallace calling from the Locater Room at the prison.

"Deane here," she said. Her face darkened.

"He did what?!"

It was the longest ten minutes the LETAC technician had ever spent.

It was bad enough having to crouch under a table in the darkness while a maniac smashed your equipment all around you. It was even worse to have to do it with your boss whining in your lap.

"Sshssshsh!" whispered the technician, with his hand over Fred Wallace's mouth. "I think he's finished."

And sure enough, it did seem that the storm was over.

Cochran wiped his brow with a handkerchief. He set down the chair he had been using as a sledgehammer and then sat down in it himself.

He lit a cigarette. He looked at his watch.

The technician looked at his watch.

A billion dollars' worth of equipment, a one-of-a-kind prototype, installed in the prison only this month, lay in ruins on the floor.

The police chief, oddly enough, was smiling.

Ten minutes after the whole thing started, the Locater Room door opened and two men came in.

"William Cochran?" one of them asked.

"Gentlemen."

"Ted Harris, sir. U.S. Marshall's office. We have orders to take you into custody for destruction of government property."

Cochran stood up and handed Harris his gun. "Do your duty, then," he said.

It was only after the marshalls had left the room with Cochran that the LETAC technician got out from under the table.

He reached back down and pulled Fred Wallace to his feet.

"You can open your eyes, sir," he said to his boss. "It's all over."

26

SUNSET IS ALWAYS BEAUTIFUL, BUT SUNSET IN A GRAVE-
yard is beautiful in a special way. It's as if, as the sky
turns over its last rosy page, the earth is closing its
book also, marking our place in the never-ending
story with the bodies of those who have gone to rest
between her dark pages.

It's a peaceful time in a peaceful place. And peace is
just what Parker Barnes needed. It was what he was
anticipating. He felt a peace that was almost like joy
as he sat in front of the tombstone he had never been
allowed to see before.

LINDA DAVIS BARNES 1961–1992

CHRISTINE MARY BARNES 1987–1992

He sensed the approach of someone, but even that
didn't break his peace, for he also sensed who it was,
and it was the one person on earth he didn't mind
sharing this moment with.

The moment of his death.

"So where's Karin's father?" he asked without turning.

There was a pause, and then he heard Madison Carter's voice. "Boston. We're divorced." She paused again. "I told Cochran about the fail-safe," Carter said after a moment. "My guess is, he's taking care of it."

"You sure?"

Carter smiled for the first time. "You're still here, aren't you?"

Barnes returned the smile as she sat beside him on the grass. "You know, this is the first time I've been here," he said. "They didn't let me come to the funeral. Linda's dad picked out the stone, God bless him."

He was suddenly conscious of Carter's eyes on the gun on his lap—the Glock he had taken from the driver of the prison van.

"Look, Madison," he said. "I'm not going back to jail. Period."

"Don't be crazy," she said. "You haven't killed anybody. We can eventually prove that. And with what you've done—how you've handled yourself, the risks you've taken. I can file my report now, and there's a good chance we'll get a sentence reduction, and—"

Barnes shook his head. "Not we, *me. I'm* the one that goes in, does the time. I've been in hell for five years and I've had it. Screw the sentence reduction. I'm not going back in. I would never get out alive anyway. These people want to be done with me; they're just looking for a reason."

"Unless you turn yourself in, every cop in L.A. will be looking for you."

Barnes shrugged. "The only chance I've got is to get

Sid 6.7, because that's the key to my freedom. And without my freedom . . ."

He looked Madison Carter in the eye. "I'd just as soon be dead. Get it?"

She looked back, and for the first time truly understood.

"I get it," she said.

The silence between them was long and wide and comfortable, as the sky slowly darkened to mauve and then to purple overhead.

It was Barnes who finally broke the spell. "How long have you been divorced?"

Carter opted to change the subject. "What if you were wrong about Sid 6.7 needing to choose a new opponent? Maybe he set you free for a reason."

Now it was Barnes's turn to change the subject. "Does your daughter miss her dad?"

Carter nodded. "Karin goes to visit him for a month every summer. She really looks forward to it. But it tears me up every time she gets on that plane. My daughter means everything to me, Parker. I don't think I'll ever get past that."

"Grimes used my daughter to get to me. And Sid 6.7 has been using my guilt about it."

"For what?" Carter looked at him quizzically, the soft mood broken.

"Just like in VR. He's been playing my pain."

Carter was beginning to follow. "He knew you could catch him. The Grimes in him knew you could, so he found your weakness, used it to throw you off balance."

"But he's not Grimes." Barnes stuck the gun into his belt and reached out a hand, pulling her to her feet. "He's interactive. He set me free because I'm not enough anymore."

"Bigger and bigger audiences. You've been right about this all along."

"I just wasn't thinking big enough."

Carter's eyes widened. "The political rally."

Barnes shook his head. "Bigger. Sid 6.7 craves feedback. He's going to go where he can get more and more of it. And I know where that is."

27

FREEDOM?" SAID THE MAN IN THE GRAY SUIT, WITH THE close-cropped gray hair. His gray eyes narrowed. "We all want freedom. What about the freedom of American citizens *not* to have their cities, their schools, their neighborhoods—and their culture!—overrun by refugees from the Third World, for whom even poverty here in the USA is preferable to the living hell of their own countries. . . ."

"Turn him down, please," said the head engineer. "Symes gives me a headache. I can watch the level on the meters without listening to his drivel."

The assistant engineer cranked down the volume. They were in the control booth of a television studio, looking at a long panel of knobs and dials under a board filled with meters and gauges under a wall studded with monitors.

On half of the monitors, the gray-suited debater, John Symes, was on live-feed from New York, expounding his theories of cultural cleanliness.

The other half of the monitors showed the other debater just outside the control-booth door, in the

Los Angeles studio: Rafael DeBaca, a tall thin Hispanic man in a brown suit, who was waiting his turn to speak.

The assistant turned up the sound when DeBaca began.

"If you close off the borders of the USA to immigration, you close off the future, you close off this country's soul and doom our children—mine and yours—to cultural extinction and—"

"Okay," said the head engineer. "Get ready to go to split screen. The lines are open and the calls are coming in."

The console board in front of the two men began flickering with the energy of millions of fiber-optic connections, of millions of opinions and prejudices, half-baked ideas and unexamined opinions, high ideals and low emotions being broken down into digits on touch-tone phones and fed into a computer that sorted them by area code, then combined the regional breakdown with the subscriber information from the national phone network database.

"Go."

The monitors all went to split screen, with one of the debaters on each side, under a headline:

NATIONAL TOWN MEETING

Interactive Debate on Immigration

A stream of figures scrolled down between the two debaters, a shimmering ribbon of opinion rippling into categories, regions, ages:

AGREE, DISAGREE
+   —
1-2-3-4-5-6-7-8-9
White Black

Hispanic
Asian
18–35
35–50
Over 50
North
South
East
Etcetera . . . .

The numbers flowed like water as each man spoke in turn, constantly changing, adjusting, modifying, up and down. It was real time. It was current. It was indecision quantified, and though it hadn't yet made its way into electoral law and replaced voting altogether, interactive opinion polling was clearly the wave of the future.

Or at least that's what the head engineer thought, as he watched the numbers shimmy and dance down the screen.

DeBaca's numbers edged up as he reminded Americans, "We have always been a nation of immigrants."

But Symes was in hot pursuit, his numbers rising as he reminded Americans, "It is not our responsibility to provide a sanctuary for the criminals and castoffs who can't make it in their own countries."

Cold data running hot. It was real!

It was realer than real.

Then something even realer came grinning through the control-room door. . . .

BLAM!

The head engineer turned just in time to see his assistant's head burst open like a seedpod in stop action, splattering red all over the knobs and dials and meters and gauges.

"Hey, I—" the head engineer began.

BLAM!

The head engineer never got to finish. He slumped gently to the floor while all his blood pumped out of the hole in his heart.

"Excuse me," said Sid 6.7, ever-so-politely nudging the body out of the way with his foot as he sat down at the control board.

First Sid 6.7 set down the laser-sighted .44 Magnum he had taken from the Olympic security guard. Then he wiped the blood and scattered tissue off the knobs and dials and meters and gauges.

Then he got to work.

"Hey, what's going on?" Rafael DeBaca asked. First there had been the noise from the control booth, two bangs almost like gunshots.

And now this.

The logo under the image on the split-screen monitors no longer read:

NATIONAL TOWN MEETING

Interactive Debate on Immigration

It read:

DEATH TV

And a voice was booming over the speakers:

"Ladies and gentlemen . . . or perhaps I should say, my fellow Americans. Welcome to the first broadcast, live from Los Angeles, of DEATH TV."

DeBaca stared at the monitors in stunned silence. His image on the split screen stared back.

Symes, on live-feed from the New York studio, was the first to react. He was outraged. "What's happening out there?" he asked. "Have we lost the West Coast?"

Rafael DeBaca turned to look behind him, toward the control booth. Behind the glass, he could see a tall, blond-haired man wearing headsets, resetting the controls, while the audio boomed.

The entertainment you've always wanted. All you have to do, sweet viewers, is ask. What do you want? Mutilation? Strangulation?"

The man in the control booth was pointing at DeBaca. There was something in his hand. DeBaca looked up toward the monitor over the booth, and saw—as millions of Americans saw—the red dot of the laser sight on his forehead.

DeBaca saw the glass of the control booth shattering, but he never heard the shot that killed him.

Light travels faster than sound.

So does a .44 Magnum bullet.

Were they too late?

The plaza in front of the MultiMedia Tower was chaos by the time Parker Barnes and Madison Carter arrived. Police were setting up lines, gawkers were sending out for sandwiches, and news crews were already staking out their anchor locations for the evening-news feeds.

Carefully avoiding the cops, Barnes approached a KDAD reporter, who was primping, getting ready for her first live-from-the-scene report.

"Has the interactive debate started?" Barnes asked.

"Started?" she said. "It's over. Some weirdo has commandeered the studio. Just shot Rafael DeBaca in the head. On live TV."

"Somebody's jamming our feed!" a technician complained from the KDAD truck.

"Parker, come here," Carter called out.

She was at the back of the KDAD van, watching the crew's nine-inch monitor. On the screen, over the DEATH TV logo, a body lay on the floor of a seemingly abandoned TV studio. A familiar face suddenly filled the screen.

A smiling face.

"Before we begin what will be the first of many, many ends," Sid 6.7 said, "a word to the parents of our younger viewers—"

The camera panned around the studio. Some of the crew were dead. Others were in the corners, tied and gagged with duct tape. The cameras were being operated by the remote in Sid 6.7's hand.

The camera panned back to Sid 6.7. "The following program will contain scenes of violence that won't be suitable for small children. . . ."

The camera panned to the floor—and in, for a tight close-up of the bullet hole in Rafael DeBaca's forehead.

"Please, let them have something to look forward to. For the rest of you won't be able to take your eyes off the screen."

"This dude is sick!" said one of the news-van technicians.

But he didn't stop watching.

And the crowd in the plaza was getting bigger all the time.

28

THE LIGHTS ON THE CONTROL BOARD WERE DANCING. The phone calls were coming in faster than ever. The scrolling figures were going up across the board, in all the demographic categories.

It was "DEATH TV" and the ratings were going through the roof.

"And now, on with the show," said Sid 6.7. His face dissolved, but the DEATH TV logo remained on video screens around the country.

Behind the logo was a high-angle scene of a small barren room, about the size of a prison cell. Jammed into the corner was what seemed to be a small bundle of clothing.

Which stirred . . . which sat up and looked around.

It was a little girl. She was bound and gagged and appeared to be crying.

"Oh, God, no—" Madison Carter cried out. The crowd gathered around the KDAD news-van monitor looked at the woman, and at the man who was holding her back, pulling her away, then they turned back to look at the drama unfolding on the screen.

A digital readout just under the DEATH TV logo read *119:43:04.*

Sid 6.7 spoke in the excited but soothing tones of a game-show host. *"Talk about jeopardy! This little beauty's got two whole hours until she gets blown to little beauty bits. And you, the viewing audience . . ."*

"You bastard! You sadistic son of a bitch!" Madison Carter broke free and lunged at the monitor on the back of the van, but Parker Barnes grabbed her again and pulled her back into the shadows. He held her in his arms as she pounded him with her fists.

"It's my fault! I should have been with her!"

"Hey!" Barnes shook her, holding her at arms' length. "It's not your fault. He was built to make this happen. Now listen to me—he's feeding on the interaction. You've got to cut the phone lines and isolate him. Can you do that?"

Tears were streaming down Carter's face. Barnes pulled her close and held her until she stopped trembling. Then he held her face between his strong dark hands and looked down into her eyes.

"I'll get Karin back. I promise."

"But . . ."

"There he is!" came a shout from behind them.

They both wheeled. SWAT cops were running across the plaza, guns drawn. "There he is! That's Barnes!"

"Go, then!" Carter pushed Barnes away, and he sprinted for the side door of the MultiMedia Tower. He was halfway across when the SWAT team ran past the news van. A cop dropped to one knee beside Carter and aimed his Mac 10 assault pistol.

Missed as Madison Carter kicked his gun, knocking the barrel upward so that it sprayed its load of death upward, into the unflinching stars.

* * *

"Barnes didn't kill anybody," said Police Chief Cochran, as he was brought into his own office by two U.S. Marshalls.

He stood facing his own desk. There in his own seat was Elizabeth Deane. Fred Wallace stood beside her, behind the desk. They were both watching something on TV.

"Sit down," Deane said.

Cochran sat down. "Parker Barnes is not a killer," he began again.

"Maybe not," said Deane. "But we have a larger problem to address."

"He didn't kill anybody and I can prove it! Now call off your goddamn dogs . . ."

"One thing at a time." Deane turned the TV around so that Cochran saw Sid 6.7's face over an unfamiliar logo.

"Death TV?"

The mall of the MultiMedia Tower was a masterpiece of modern architecture, cunningly constructed to give the illusion that there were no definite boundaries between outside and inside; it was seductively designed to lead the eye inward from the street (now hopelessly jammed with emergency vehicles and police cars), across the wide central plaza (now covered with snaking cables, panicked spectators, and nervous cops), and into the vast two-story glass-enclosed lower lobby of the building itself—a lobby that was now empty except for one man, an African-American who was running at breakneck speed behind a row of potted plants, toward the black marble security desk between the elevators.

The inside and outside of the building were separated by a wall of glass. Clear, perfect, flawless thermopane, as invisible, under the best of conditions, as air. This evening, however, conditions weren't the best. At least for glass. The two-story-tall lobby panes of the MultiMedia Tower were making what might have been called their first and last public appearance, shattering in sheets under the hail of bullets aimed at the man fleeing across the lobby. It was almost like Zen poetry. The glass became visible only as it fell; it fully appeared only in the act of disappearing.

The same might be said of the fugitive who leaped over the last row of plants and disappeared behind the security desk.

When Barnes hit the floor behind the security desk, he saw how Sid. 6.7 had gotten into the building.

The security guard, a slightly overweight black man, lay on his stomach, his blind eyes looking upward, his neck twisted at an improbable angle.

Barnes closed the man's eyes.

The wood at the top of the desk was flying into splinters, chipped away by the rain of fire from the cautiously approaching SWAT teams.

The elevator was standing open, only twenty feet away. But it was twenty feet of open floor.

While Barnes checked the clip on his Glock, he thought about returning fire—just a few rounds to slow the SWAT teams down. Then he rejected the idea. He was still a cop; he wasn't about to start shooting at cops.

Not even shooting back.

Barnes thought about using the security guard for a shield. They would think he was a hostage. Then he rejected the idea. Security guards wore uniforms but they were civilians, and he wasn't about to start hiding behind civilians.

Not even dead civilians.

The shooting had stopped. The sudden silence gave Barnes an idea. He placed his foot against the security guard's chair and gave it a kick. It went rolling across the marble floor, away from the elevators.

BADABADABAD!

POPOPOPOP!

RATATATATA!

All hell broke loose. And while it was still breaking, Barnes flung himself out from behind the desk, across the open floor and into the elevator, hitting CLOSE as he flattened himself against the wall, breathing a sigh of relief as the door extended itself like a protective glove to stop the rain of bullets from the approaching SWAT teams.

"Okay, Sid 6.7," muttered Barnes. "Now, what floor?"

29

*E*VEN CHAOS HAS ITS PERFECTION, AND THE CHAOS IN and around the ground floor of the MultiMedia Tower was almost perfect. The street was choked with cars and trucks. The plaza was filled with civilians and rubberneckers. The LAPD and federal SWAT teams had argued, since losing Barnes into the elevator, about whether he was a primary or a secondary target, or even a target at all (one LAPD officer claimed he was still a cop under deep cover). While they argued, one of them flipped a coin to decide which team would start up the stairwell and which would commandeer an elevator.

Outside, at the temporary command post set up in the plaza, the captain of the Joint Task Force was on the phone. It was being confirmed for him by the highest authority that the rogue-cop Parker Barnes was, indeed, a primary target, along with the kidnapper-killer in the studio on the top floor.

Both were STK, or shoot-to-kill.

"Yes ma'am," the captain said. *Whatever you say, Crime Queen.*

The captain hung up his cellular phone. *Be glad when this is over,* he thought. *Wish Cochran was here. He's better at this sort of business than I am.*

He looked up when he heard a welcome sound:

WHUMP WHUMP WHUMP

The Bell-Colt helicopter gunship, sent by the state from Sacramento, was arriving. *That'll be a help,* the captain thought. *But only if they come out on the roof.*

He sent orders to the pilot to hover, guns at the ready.

Dr. Madison Carter stood in the crowd, hitting redial on a borrowed cellular phone, over and over.

It had taken everything she'd had, including her LETAC ID, her police pass, her press pass, and her most apologetic smile—aided by the fact that the SWAT team had been in a hurry—to convince the captain that her interference with the officer aiming at Parker Barnes had been an accident.

Now she was waiting and watching like everyone else, doing the only thing she could think of to do: trying to cut off Sid 6.7's interactive phone lines. But it didn't seem to be enough. Karin was Sid 6.7's captive somewhere, maybe in the basement, maybe not even in this building!

She tried to think of someone else to call. Someone with a computer, who could . . .

Suddenly, across the plaza, she saw a familiar face in the crowd of rubberneckers behind the police barriers.

Lindenmeyer.

Madison Carter started to alert the captain, then thought better of the idea. What would they do but arrest Lindenmeyer? She needed information from him.

She reached into her purse and found the little Walther PPK .380 she'd taken from her bedside table. Clicking off the safety, she started across the plaza, weaving though the crowd.

47.

48.

Parker Barnes had a theory. Always start at the top.

49.

50.

Ding.

The theory paid off. When the elevator door opened, Barnes saw a flashing light over a door at the end of the corridor.

The door was marked STUDIO B.

The flashing red light read ON THE AIR.

The door was locked.

Barnes lowered his nine mm Glock toward the knob.

"DEATH TV" was a winner; Sid 6.7 could see that.

The show was breaking records as the live-feed went out to every TV station, satellite, and relay in the world. Numbers don't lie, and the figures scrolling down between the split-screen images showed more discretional viewers than any real-life live TV extravaganza since the O.J. Simpson Bronco chase. The stream of statistics flowed, constantly changing. The ratings continued to rise, the demographics got broader, the approval statistics cut across all barriers of age, race, sex, area code.

And no wonder! Sid 6.7 thought. The monitors on the studio wall showed the split-screen signal that was going out coast to coast. The left side of the screen showed a little girl, sobbing in a tiny dark cell-like room. The readout underneath her read: *the precious moments left.* A pathetic scene, to be sure. But the other side made up for it.

The right half of the split screen showed Sid 6.7 in all his glory. His blond hair was shining. His blue eyes were glittering like little chips of sky. His teeth were gleaming in a wide smile, as he strutted among his hostages, gun in one hand and the remote control for the cameras in the other. All that was missing was the karaoke soundtrack!

But this was even better. This was prime time; this was coast to coast.

Sid 6.7 was in heaven.

Literally. America was witnessing the ascension into paradise of a digital being.

"Think of it!" Sid 6.7 announced as he strutted ecstatically. "This little girl is going to die. I'll say it again. This little girl will be dead 100 minutes from now."

The robotic video camera followed Sid 6.7 as he strolled, chin in hand, through the studio, examining the terrified hostages who were huddled against the wall. Then he smiled at the camera lens once again.

"And there isn't anything that she, or anyone else, can do to stop that," Sid 6.7 said.

He sat down in a chair, the ultimate talk-show host. "We've got a great show tonight. Don't we, Ed?"

He pointed his gun at one of the terrified hostages.

On the monitors, the stream of numbers danced and shimmered. The promise of a live execution was sending the ratings soaring even higher. Narrowing his eyes in a prayer of thankfulness, Sid 6.7 began to squeeze the trigger.

Then he opened them abruptly as the numbers disappeared.

He jumped to his feet angrily. "What the hell happened to the phone lines?!"

KRAK!

"What the . . ." It wasn't Sid 6.7's gun; he hadn't fired yet. The shot had come from behind him.

KRAK!

Sid 6.7 turned just in time to see the studio door fly open and Parker Barnes rush through, firing.

KRAK!

KRAK!

Sid 6.7 ducked behind the camera and opened fire in return. "Mr. Parker Barnes! Mr. Nine Lives! Welcome to Death TV!"

"DEATH TV" was a winner; Fred Wallace could see that. The sobbing little girl, the strutting maniac . . . it was hard to watch, but it was even harder to turn away.

Numbers don't lie, and the figures scrolling down between the split-screen images showed more discretional viewers than any real-life live TV extravaganza since the Waco incineration.

The promise of a live execution had sent the ratings soaring even higher, and now, with an actual firefight in progress in a studio . . .

Elizabeth Deane and Wallace saw it all on the TV in Police Chief Cochran's office.

Cochran missed it, though. He was on the phone.

He hung up and turned to Wallace and Deane, elated by the news he had just heard.

"That was the lab. They confirm that the two prison guards and the woman on the train were killed by the .44 Sid 6.7 was carrying. Now if we can only find Parker before . . ."

"Shit—isn't that Parker—he's in there, with Sid!" sputtered Wallace. He pointed at the television.

Suddenly half the screen went dark. The little girl on the left was still there, over the time readout. But the right half, the Sid 6.7 half, was dark.

"What happened?!" protested Fred Wallace, along with 89.7 million other Americans. He was disappointed.

Cochran smiled with satisfaction. "They've taken Sid offline."

Sid 6.7 stood—just in time to see Parker Barnes in the doorway, his Glock in hand. Barnes was back and there was no way out, except . . .

Sid 6.7 looked up toward the ceiling, covered with flimsy panels. He leaped and crashed through, catching a steel beam, and with one hand, using his nano-strength, he pulled himself up into the crawl space.

KRAK!

KRAK!

Sid 6.7 laughed. Barnes was firing, but wildly. His shots made holes in the ceiling, and the holes let through light, and the spots of light looked like stars, and Sid 6.7 was starting to feel like he was in heaven again.

He leaped from beam to beam, laughing, until he found a catwalk that led to a doorway.

KRAK!

Sid 6.7 stopped laughing when one of Barnes's lucky shots shattered his knee. He dragged himself onto the catwalk. It led to a door and into a stairwell.

Sid 6.7 shut the door behind him and looked up the stairs. There was no glass here, only synthetic blood pumping out and reddening the steps. The stairway led up to a steel door.

It was locked, and Sid 6.7 was getting weaker. He had to use both hands.

He twisted off the knob. He yanked loose the chain. He kicked the door open.

30

IT WAS BEAUTIFUL. IT WAS MAYHEM.

Poets can't be trusted with public policy, the poet W. H. Auden once said, because they "adore explosions." Poets like "thunderstorms, tornados, conflagrations, ruins, and scenes of spectacular carnage."

Add to that, murder and mayhem.

And it was true. Lindenmeyer was a poet. A digital poet. A bard of code (and what is language but code?), a balladeer of the personality profile and the module.

And that was his poem up there. Sid 6.7. A perfect blend of the Top 200 serial killers—a walking, talking hit parade of horror.

The pity was, no one knew it.

As far as anyone could tell, Lindenmeyer was just one of the crowd: one of the slobbering, wide-eyed rubberneckers who crowded against the police lines, watching and marveling at the poetic "scenes of spectacular carnage" being unleashed in the TV studios of the MultiMedia Tower.

No one knew that Daryl Lindenmeyer was the Dante who had created this magnificent hell.

Lindenmeyer had no doubt that the forces assembling in the plaza would eventually bring Sid 6.7 down. Not even the ultimate serial killer could prevail against the combined firepower of the LAPD, the Highway Patrol, the National Guard, and Elizabeth Deane's federal SWAT teams.

But that was all right. So what if they killed this Sid? Lindenmeyer had plenty of other copies. Sid 6.7 was much better than a human. He was binary, he was digital; he was replicable. He could be copied, altered, improved upon. There would be other Sids, upgrades, higher versions, maybe even . . .

"Where is she?"

Lindenmeyer's first reaction was to be pissed off that someone would so rudely interrupt his thoughts. He started to turn around and give that someone hell, but something told him not to.

That something was the cold steel barrel of a gun pressed against the back of his neck.

Lindenmeyer raised his hands. He thought it was the cops. Then he heard the voice again.

"Where's my daughter?"

"Please, Dr. Carter . . ." Lindenmeyer turned slowly, so as not to alarm her; he lowered his voice to a whimper. "I don't know. On my honor . . ."

Striking swiftly, he grabbed the barrel of the Walther and wrenched it upward. He bent back the little woman's thumb. It was a great feeling, *to be like Sid!*

"And I wouldn't tell you if I did, you little bi—"

The word was cut short by Carter's fist, a right cross to the chin, knocking Lindenmeyer's glasses off and sending a tooth flying back into his throat.

He fell to his knees. He swallowed; he gagged.

He threw up.

When Lindenmeyer opened his eyes, the crowd was

roaring, looking up. No one noticed the gun in his ear, or if they did, they thought it was a lovers' quarrel.

Madison Carter's whisper was as soft, as harsh, as cold as death itself.

"Then we'll have to ask Sid 6.7. Let's go!"

The fifty-two-story MultiMedia Tower was the third tallest building in Los Angeles, and its flat rooftop commanded a view that stretched from the Pacific in the west, to the mountains in the north, to the desert in the east; and in between, it overlooked a varicolored city that looked in the daytime like a chunky smog soup, but at night, like a tray of loose diamonds.

Unfortunately, even though it was night, little of this beauty could be seen directly from the roof. Due to insurance concerns, the entire rooftop was sealed in by a twenty-foot-high wall of rather dirty glass. An automatic window-washing machine was being installed at one end of the roof, but it wasn't yet operational.

The purpose of the glass was not only to protect the owners of the MultiMedia Tower from lawsuits by the relatives of suicides (a burgeoning litigational subspecies), but also to protect the three air-conditioning towers on the roof from the sand-and-dust-laden desert winds.

These three round windowless towers, each twelve feet high and six feet in diameter, were spaced in a triangle on the flat roof. In the center of the three was a wedge-shaped stairway entrance with a steel door.

The door was locked, bolted, and chained.

Almost an impediment to Sid 6.7.

The service-stairway door burst open and Sid 6.7 emerged onto the roof, running with a limp, favoring his shattered knee. Breaking down the door had taken more out of him than he had anticipated.

Getting weaker . . .

He scooped up a handful of gravel from the roof, but it didn't help.

Glass. He needed glass. The food of the gods.

The stairwell door creaked open, and Sid 6.7 saw Barnes peering and then diving through.

KRAK!

KRAK!

Close! *Should have locked the door behind me,* Sid 6.7 thought. The game was getting close.

Sid 6.7 ducked behind one of the three air-conditioning towers. He reached around with his .44 Magnum and fired wildly.

BLAM!

BLAM!

click

Empty! That was another problem with the real world. In VR, you didn't run out of ammunition, or if you did, you simply reset. Here you had to . . .

KRAK!

KRAK!

click

Voilà! Barnes's Glock was empty, too. Maybe for good this time. Sid 6.7 smiled. The odds were getting better. *I might even make it back to heaven,* he thought.

Then he heard another, unfamiliar sound:

WHUMP

WHUMP

WHUMP

31

*F*LYING A HELICOPTER FROM POINT TO POINT IS EASY. IT'S standing still that's hard.

Jack Yancey was getting dizzy. The human brain is made for movement; for short data bursts; for quick scans of passing landmarks, instant equilibrium adjustments; for fast breaks and sudden fakes. But hovering in one place, trying to stay exactly a hundred meters above and a hundred due north of the Multi-Media Tower, required a total concentration that was making Jack dizzy, as dizzy as spinning in place would have made him as a kid.

Cats are good at sitting and waiting, Jack thought. *They should train a cat to fly this thing. Not an evolved primate like me.*

And a cat could have almost done it. The Bell-Colt X-2232 was the latest high-tech weapons platform. With its twin .50 caliber computer-controlled guns, it was like a machine gun with a brain, plus a driver.

Jack was the driver. All the driver had to do was put

the copter in the target area, and the computer did the rest.

Maybe I'll bring a cat with me next time, Jack thought. *Teach it to . . .*

KRAK!

KRAK!

And then, there it was! Gunshots on the roof. Grinning, Jack dropped the Bell-Colt a few feet, spun, and circled in toward the glassed-in top of the Multi-Media Tower.

Show Time.

He punched ENTER and took his hands off the controls. He felt the Bell-Colt swing in smaller and smaller arcs as the heat-seeking sensors scanned the rooftop of the building, searching for targets.

But what was taking so long? Jack could already see the targets. Two guys dodging around the towers on the roof, one of them shooting. The computer was taking too long to find them and fire.

Then Jack realized why. The glass enclosure was dissipating the heat signal, complicating the feedback loop that aimed and locked and fired the guns, confusing the computer.

So much for cutting-edge technology! By the time the computer figured it out, the fugitives would be dead, or gone, or both.

Jack hit OVERRIDE. He would take out the glass himself. Maybe even take out the guys. It didn't matter which one. According to the boss lady, they both were targets. Both STK.

Jack hit FIRE.

BADADADADADADA!

BADADADADADADA!

Parker Barnes hit the dirt, or rather, the gravel and asphalt of the roof.

Gunshots were clanging off the air-conditioning tower over his head and kicking up the gravel at his feet. The musical sound of shattering glass filled the air, above the drumbeat of the guns. And under it all was the soft bass

WHUMP WHUMP WHUMP

of the helicopter gunship moving in, closer and closer.

BADADADADADADA!

BADADADADADADA!

Sid 6.7 dove across the open space between two of the air-conditioning towers, barely ahead of the bullets that stitched a line of craters in the asphalt-and-gravel roof.

He was being shot at from the helicopter now. As if Barnes wasn't trouble enough. But every cloud has a silver lining—or even better, a diamond lining.

And there was the diamond-like glitter of glass in the gravel at his feet! And there was the heavenly, musical sound of breaking glass.

Glass.

The food of the gods.

BADADADADADADA!

BADADADADADADA!

Jack Yancey pulled up, smiling with satisfaction. Some jobs it still took a human to do. Now that a section of the glass wall was gone, the computer would be able to find and lock on the targets on the rooftop.

Both were clearly visible. The big blond guy was limping across the rooftop, and if Jack hadn't known better, he would have sworn he was scooping up broken glass and eating it.

The second fugitive, the black guy, was chasing him.

It would be easy to take them both out at once, Jack thought. He seriously considered leaving the guns on OVERRIDE and doing it himself.

Then he decided against it. Too many forms to fill out.

Let the computer blow them away. He punched in AUTO and hit ENTER.

"Call him off! Call him off!" screamed the man jumping off the back of the motorcycle, which had woven through the gridlocked traffic and then ridden over the curb and up the steps, directly into the plaza of the MultiMedia Tower.

The captain of the Joint Task Force didn't notice the motorcycle until the last moment. "How did that crazy get past our lines?" he asked his lieutenant.

"Call him off!" the man repeated, now on foot, running across the plaza.

The captain was about to have him stopped, or shot, or worse—but there was something familiar about the voice.

"Get that copter away from there. Call him off!"

It was Police Chief Cochran.

"I'm taking over here. Deane's orders. We have new information . . ."

With an audible sigh of relief, the captain saluted and took out his cellular phone. He punched in a number and handed the phone to Cochran with a smile.

"Copter driver's name's Yancey," he said.

* * *

187

Fifty-two stories above, the Bell-Colt X-2232 swung away from the rooftop, hovered a moment, and then swooped down toward the street. The long looping lines of its retreat seemed almost to suggest disappointment.

32

TWO PISTOLS LAY ON THE ROOFTOP OF THE MULTIMEDIA
Tower.

A Ruger .44 Magnum.

A Glock nine mm.

Both empty, both discarded.

Sid 6.7 ran across the rooftop, between the air-
conditioning towers. He knelt and scooped up glass as
he ran, but it was not enough. Synthetic blood was
streaming out of his shattered knee and still pumping
out of the hole in his chest.

"Where is she?" Parker Barnes called out, running
after him. "Tell me where the girl is . . ."

"Not the same, Barnes," Sid 6.7 said, using a
dangling electrical cord to swing upward, scrambling
to the top of one of the air-conditioning towers. "Not
your daughter . . ."

Sid 6.7 tried to think of a devastating and appropri-
ate taunt, but his nano-cells were in repair, not
thought mode—and anyway, it was hard to think
with air whistling in and out of the holes in his chest.

Damn! Barnes was scrambling up the electrical line.

Sid 6.7 leaped across to the top of the next air-conditioning tower.

Damn! Barnes was right behind him.

It was time to stop and fight. But it was getting harder to concentrate. And fighting was no fun without a gun.

No gun, no fun!

Giggling, his head spinning, Sid 6.7 jumped to the next tower.

From here, it was only a ten-foot jump to the scaffolding where the automatic window washer was installed on its grid of steel tracks, waiting to be tested.

Sid 6.7 jumped.

When he hit the scaffolding it swayed—out over the edge of the building—then fell back into place with a clank.

Here at the edge of the scaffolding, the glass was intact. Sid 6.7 bit out a crescent-shaped bite, just to hear the delicious crunch.

Food of the gods!

From fifty stories above the street, Sid 6.7 could see the whole city of Los Angeles, and a beautiful city it was—all glass and light, all violence and laughter and cybernetic dreams. He took another bite of the glass. He was beginning to feel better already!

Damn! There was Parker Barnes, on the third air-conditioning tower.

"Where is she, you bastard?" Barnes called out angrily. Then he jumped toward the scaffold.

That was his mistake.

Sid 6.7 stepped aside gracefully; he was already starting to glow with new energy from the glass. He extended one foot as Barnes hit the scaffolding, and Barnes tripped and fell, sprawling. Dazed.

Aha! Sid 6.7 grabbed Barnes by the neck and pulled him out, over the edge of the glass, to the razor-sharp tracks of the automated window-washing machine. *Steel wheels!*

He laid Barnes's neck across the track.

Ready to slice!

Make it run! Sid 6.7 reached into the window washer's control box and ripped out a handful of wires. He squeezed them in his fingers until sparks flew, until the window washer's motor groaned and whined to life, and the machine began trundling eagerly toward Barnes's outstretched neck.

GGGNNNNGGGGG . . .

Sid 6.7 smiled. "This one," he said, "is for me!"

GGGGNNNNNGGGNNNNGGNNN . . .

When Barnes came to, the first thing he saw was Sid 6.7's beautiful sky-blue eyes. Then he looked up and saw Sid 6.7's brilliant, sharp white teeth.

Then Barnes felt Sid 6.7's regenerating nano-synthetic fingers around his throat. Then he felt the cold steel of the track against the back of his neck.

Then he heard the whine of the approaching window-washing machine, and he realized he had one, and only one, chance for survival.

And that involved a suicide attempt.

Barnes wrapped his left arm around the cable of the window-washing machine. With his right hand, he grabbed Sid 6.7's belt. Then he threw his feet up and flipped himself backward, over the top of the scaffolding and into the air fifty stories above the street.

"Aaaaaahhhh!" Was that his scream, or Sid 6.7's? Barnes didn't know. All he knew was that he was falling.

He wasn't sure the cable would hold until he felt the pull, the jerk, and then the slow acceleration as he and Sid 6.7 swung back, faster and faster, toward the glass.

At the last moment, Barnes managed to twist around so that Sid 6.7 hit first. Closing his eyes and hoping for the best, Barnes followed through the shower of shattered glass. He hit asphalt and rolled, slamming with a thud against the side of an air-conditioning tower.

Still hoping for the best, Barnes opened his eyes.

Sid 6.7 was lying in a pile of broken glass. He was thrashing as if he were having a fit, convulsing like Donovan when he had died in the VR pod.

Behind Sid 6.7, in the center of the roof, someone had just kicked open the steel door of the service stairwell again.

Daryl Lindenmeyer stumbled out, gasping for breath.

Dr. Madison Carter was right behind him, holding a pistol to the back of his head.

"Parker . . ."

Barnes gave Carter a hug, surprised at how right she felt in his arms, and together they dragged the reluctant Lindenmeyer over to the pile of broken glass, where Sid 6.7 was writhing and convulsing.

Sid 6.7 looked bad. Shards and spears of shattered glass were sticking out of his chest, his neck, the ruins of his once-handsome face. One arm had been sliced off and lay flooping like a fish between his legs. His hair was twisting like a mass of snakes. There was a fist-size hole in the side of his head, and blood was running out of it—and being sucked up by another grapefruit-size hole in his abdomen. He was laughing; no, moaning; no, howling; no . . .

"What the hell's going on?" Barnes demanded.

"Silicon overload," said Lindenmeyer, shrugging. "The software's okay, but the hardware's running amok. Too much stimulus for Reilly's stupid nano-molecular assemblers."

As they watched, Sid 6.7 continued to morph, to modulate, to evolve. Always before, his features and expressions had changed, reflecting the 183 personalities in his character module; now it was his entire body that changed—sprouting hair, growing new limbs, casting off grotesque protuberances and cancerous growths as the nano-cells regenerated wildly.

It was like watching a creature speeded up in time—a hideous being, part infant, part ancient, all monster.

Sid 6.7 only had one eye left—an eye as big as an egg, shot through with streaks of red and watery clouds of white. He looked up at Lindenmeyer pleadingly, almost worshipfully.

Was that a tear? Barnes wondered.

Barnes came closer to the misshapen face. "Tell me where the girl is!"

Sid 6.7's "mouth," or what was left of it, seemed to move and Barnes leaned in—only to feel Sid 6.7's fingers clamp around his throat, squeezing tighter and tighter. He couldn't breathe.

His vision graying, Barnes found himself staring at the back of Sid 6.7's head—or, rather, at a squarish bump protruding under a clear portion of skin at the base of the skull. Abruptly, Barnes realized what it was. And what he had to do.

Barnes raised his artificial hand and drove it into Sid 6.7's head, splitting it open. He searched around with his fingers, then at last he found what he was looking for. A second later, his hand emerged with the plastic character module.

Sid 6.7 went limp. His one eye closed; his body stopped changing; it collapsed into itself like a fire going out.

Lindenmeyer looked on blankly. Carter's expression was equally numb. "We can't find her now," she said softly. "We can't find her."

Barnes wiped the gore off the "SID 6.7" module and stared at it, then at Lindenmeyer.

Maybe we can, he thought.

33

SID 6.7 SMILED. "THIS ONE," HE SAID, "IS FOR ME!"
GGGGNNNNNGGGNNNNGGNNN . . .

When Barnes came to, the first thing he saw was Sid 6.7's beautiful sky-blue eyes. Then he looked up and saw Sid 6.7's brilliant, sharp white teeth.

Then Barnes felt Sid 6.7's regenerating nano-synthetic fingers around his throat. Then he felt the cold steel of the track against the back of his neck.

Then he heard the whine of the approaching window-washing machine, and he realized he had one, and only one, chance for survival.

And that involved a suicide attempt.

Barnes threw his feet up and flipped himself backward, over the top of the scaffolding and into the air fifty stories above the street.

"AAAAAaaaaahhhhhhhh!"

In the movies, the screams of someone falling always get softer and softer, dimmer and dimmer, as they fall. *This is different,* Barnes realized, as he turned and twisted in the air. In the movies, the scream is always being heard by someone who is not falling, someone left standing on the rooftop or the top of the cliff. In the movies, the scream itself is falling, getting farther and farther away, literally dropping in volume and pitch and intensity.

But when you are the one screaming, when you are the one falling, the scream stays the same.

"AAAAAAAHHHHH!"

It might even get a little louder as it echoes back up at you from the street.

Then it stops.

All of a sudden.

"Parker!"

Madison Carter stood by the open stairwell door, listening, horrified, as Barnes's screams faded.

And faded and faded.

She winced as she heard the soft, faraway thud. And then the awful silence.

"Don't worry about him," came a familiar voice behind her.

Carter turned and screamed when she saw those sky-blue eyes, that gleaming smile. It was Sid 6.7.

She raised the Walther PPK .380 and fired directly into his face, but Sid 6.7 ducked so that the bullet only took off a little chunk of his brow.

It immediately started forming again.

"Go ahead," said Sid 6.7. "Try it again. Do it! You can't kill me!"

Better than ever! Sid 6.7 thought. *I love real life. Real guns going off, real people to kill.*

He grabbed Carter, reveling in the feel of her soft flesh beneath his nano-sensitive fingers, and he began dragging her toward one of the air-conditioning cylinders.

"Where is she?" Carter screamed. "Where's Karin? Where's my daughter?"

"Waiting."

The cars slowed and swerved to avoid hitting the crumpled body in the middle of the street. They were all new models. Nobody honked or stopped. A few pedestrians walked by on the sidewalk, not noticing, or pretending not to notice, the slight commotion in the street.

The blood pooled outward from Barnes's smashed skull, puddling into a little lake on the glistening asphalt. Then it pulled back, as if it were being sucked back into his head.

Parker Barnes opened his eyes. He got up and brushed himself off, then ran, faster and faster, across the street, into the lobby of the MultiMedia Tower. The police stood aside to let him through.

"Okay, you're reset," said Lindenmeyer. He was seated in front of a computer terminal in his old familiar office deep inside the LETAC complex. The character module slotted into the computer console read SID 6.7.

"It's working?"

"It's working," Lindenmeyer said. "Sid 6.7 assumes he's still in the real world."

"Good," said Police Chief Cochran. He was standing behind Lindenmeyer with his gun held casually in his hand. It was no longer aimed at the back of Lindenmeyer's head. It wasn't necessary. Lindenmeyer was nothing if not cooperative.

In the background, Carter and Barnes were suspended side by side in the skeletal Virtual Reality pods. Their eyes were closed. They looked like they were sleeping. *Almost like newlyweds,* Cochran thought.

"Show me Parker again," he said.

Lindenmeyer hit the keyboard. The big-screen monitor on the wall showed Barnes in the lobby of the MultiMedia Tower, hitting the elevator button. As usual in VR, an elevator was waiting, ready to go.

"Now show me Sid 6.7 and Dr. Carter."

Lindenmeyer toggled the display sequence.

The monitor showed Madison Carter's face pressed against the cold steel of an air-conditioning cylinder on the roof. She was screaming.

"Tell me where my daughter is!"

"You *really* want to know?" Sid 6.7 asked. He was cackling, he was crackling, he was electrified with evil energy. "Do you *really?* Just click your heels three times, like this!"

He knocked on the cold steel of the air-conditioning cylinder. "Oh, Karin?" he called sweetly.

"She's in there? She's been right in there all along?"

Sid raised his eyebrows in an exaggerated gesture of concern and amazement. "Why, yes, Auntie Em!"

"Madison! Stand back!"

Sid 6.7 looked toward the stairwell door, and his look of mock amazement turned to real amazement—or at least to VR amazement.

Parker Barnes was running across the rooftop.

"You're dead!" Sid 6.7 protested.

"I'm playing an encore," Barnes called out. He looked up toward the sky, "Got what we need, Billy. Now get us out of here, fast!"

Cochran nudged Lindenmeyer with the gun. "How do I get them out?"

"Just release the pods," Lindenmeyer said. "Lower them from the ceiling, then take the helmets off. I need to stay here at the console and watch the sensitivity levels. We don't want another disaster like . . ."

"Yeah, yeah . . ."

Cochran ran back to find the control panel for the VR pods, and Lindenmeyer turned back to his console.

Meanwhile, Sid 6.7's face was in close-up on the big-screen monitor. Huge. Confused.

Then enraged.

Betrayed! "I'm back in VR!" Sid 6.7 screamed.

"Smart, smart," whispered Lindenmeyer. "That's my guy."

He turned Barnes's sensitivity level up. Way up.

"Which one lowers which pod?" Cochran called out to Lindenmeyer. There were two rows of levers on the wall.

Cochran pulled a lever and nothing happened.

He pulled another lever, and one of the VR pods began to lower, with a soft electrical whine.

Carter's.

"Found one of them!" Cochran said. *Now which one worked Parker's pod?*

Cochran was so intent on looking that he didn't hear Lindenmeyer get up from his seat in front of the computer.

Didn't hear him stalk across the room.

Didn't hear him pick up a piece of pipe from the workbench.

Cochran didn't hear anything until the pipe smashed against the side of his head. And then he heard just one final sound, like a bell ringing too loud, too close.

And then silence.

Cochran lay crumpled on the floor, his blood pooling by his smashed skull. Lindenmeyer looked down and shook his head and smiled sadly.

"Sorry, Chief, no reset this time," he said. "This is the real world."

"Aaaaggghhhh!"

Lindenmeyer raced back to his computer terminal. Sid 6.7's face still filled the big-screen monitor on the wall, larger and more furious than ever.

"I'm back in the box!" Sid 6.7 screamed. Behind him, Carter and Barnes could be seen backing away, waiting to be snatched out of VR.

Suddenly Carter disappeared from Barnes's side. The rooftop of the MultiMedia Tower began to vibrate and sway. The mysteriously restored glass began to shatter and fall again, all around the edge of the rooftop. Lindenmeyer watched, transfixed, as Sid's rage began to buckle and warp the virtual universe. In the background, the buildings on the horizon began to shake as if in a 9.9 earthquake.

"Awesome!" said Lindenmeyer, staring at the computer.

"If I can't leave, neither will you!" Sid 6.7 yelled at Barnes. He screamed with the thunderous rage of an insane God, and Barnes was thrown as if by a wind toward the edge of the building—and over the side again.

"Awesome," Lindenmeyer whispered. He toggled a command on the keyboard, upping his sensitivity level to eight hundred percent and watched Barnes fall, and fall, and fall. . . .

34

WITH A PRODIGIOUS EFFORT OF WILL THAT WAS ALMOST like waking herself out of a dream, Madison Carter ripped off her skull cap and sat up in the VR pod. At first she wasn't sure she was back in the real world.

She saw Cochran, lying on the floor in a pool of his own blood.

She saw Lindenmeyer across the room at a keyboard, gloating and chuckling to himself.

She saw a body on the big-screen monitor, twisting and falling through the air.

She heard a noise and saw Barnes above her, still in his VR pod. He was bucking and thrashing, as if he were having an epileptic fit.

"Parker!" She stepped out of her pod and ran to the wall. She pulled all the release levers down at once, and Barnes's VR pod began to descend.

But slowly. Too slowly.

"AAAAAAAHHHHH!"

Parker Barnes was falling. Hurtling down through

fifty stories of empty air toward the street. Again. But this time the pavement as it rushed up toward him was shimmering, rippling like water, wavering. . . .

Barnes closed his eyes, prepared to hear the awful silence at the end of his long scream, but this time there was nothing. No stop. No splat. No silence.

This time he fell through the street.

He felt his molecules expand and come apart as they brushed past the expanding molecules of the asphalt and the earth, all shifting and shimmering in the storm of Sid 6.7's fury. Falling through the street was like falling through a cloud.

It was a peaceful, easy feeling.

"Parker!" Carter pleaded. "Can you hear me?"

The skeletal VR pod whined as it lowered to the floor and opened. Barnes had stopped thrashing.

He looked dead.

Carter reached down to pull the VR helmet off his head, when she heard a voice behind her.

"Stay away from him!"

It was Lindenmeyer.

"It's a new experiment," Lindenmeyer said with a cold grin. "I have the sensitivity turned all the way up, off the scale. Barnes is going all the way."

"All the way?"

"Into subatomic space. The ultimate Virtual Reality trip, into the ultimate void. And it's one-way!"

Barnes was falling through the world.

Falling through the stones that made up the world.

Falling through the molecules that made up the stones.

Falling through the atoms that made up the molecules.

The atoms spun and danced around one another like planets, then they too were gone, as far away as galaxies, and there was only the singing.

The singing. It was the force that held the universe together.

There was no down, no up. There was only the singing—and a darkness so wonderfully complete that matter itself was only a hole in it.

And Barnes was still falling. . . .

"I said, don't touch him!" Lindenmeyer yelled.

Ignoring him, Carter was trying to rip off Barnes's VR helmet before it was too late. She looked up just in time to see Lindenmeyer advancing toward her with the steel pipe in his hand. It was still shiny with Cochran's blood.

But Carter had a weapon of her own. The Walther PPK.

She didn't know where to aim, so she aimed at Lindenmeyer's right eye, huge behind a thick lens.

BLAM!

The right lens of the glasses disappeared, and so did the eye. Carter turned back to the pod and the VR helmet.

She had it off Barnes's head before Lindenmeyer's lifeless body had hit the floor.

The world was back.

Parker Barnes sat up in his opened VR pod, still dazed.

The world was back, and what a world! Sid 6.7 was on the big-screen monitor, still screaming with impotent rage. Madison Carter was standing beside the pod with the gun in her hand. And there, on the floor . . .

Dizzily, Barnes sat up and pulled himself out of the pod. He stepped across Lindenmeyer's body and knelt beside Police Chief Cochran. He gently closed his friend's eyes.

"Thanks, Billy. Thanks for everything."

He was still wobbly. Madison Carter helped him stand. "Now, we have to get Karin!" she pleaded.

Suddenly the door to the lab burst open, and Fred Wallace stormed in, followed by Elizabeth Deane.

"I don't know what you two are doing here," he began, "but this is private property, and you are not—"

His speech was cut short by the steel-and-plastic hammer of Parker Barnes's left fist, slamming into his face.

"Tell me what you two need," said Elizabeth Deane, trying to hide her pleased smile.

"We need to get to the MultiMedia Tower, the top, on the double," said Barnes.

"Then let's go," said Deane. "I have a helicopter outside in the parking lot."

Barnes started to follow Deane and Carter out the door, then noticed that the big-screen monitor had gone dark. He stopped at Lindenmeyer's computer console and hit a key.

The video came up; the monitor on the wall showed Karin in her dark cell. The time display underneath read:

11:06:23

Karin had stopped crying. She was huddled on a mat, either sleeping, or—or worse.

Barnes hit another key, changing the video display. Sid 6.7 was still screaming from the VR screen.

"It's time somebody shut you up," Barnes said.

He popped the "SID 6.7" module out of the slot and stuck it into his pocket, then headed out the door after Carter and Deane.

35

PARKER BARNES WAS OUT OF THE HELICOPTER BEFORE
the skid had even touched down on the asphalt and
gravel roof of the MultiMedia Tower.

"Good luck!" said Jack Yancey, never dreaming
that Barnes was the same man he had tried to kill a
half-hour before.

"Parker, wait up . . ."

Madison Carter was right behind Barnes. They ran
across the rooftop, trying to orient themselves and
figure out which of the three air-conditioning cylinders held Karin.

Then Barnes heard the knocking.

"Karin?"

There it was again.

He knocked on the small service port, low and
narrow, like a doorway for a child.

"Karin?"

"Mommy!"

"Karin!" Madison Carter lunged around Barnes,
reaching for the door.

Barnes grabbed her arm and pulled her back. "Don't," he said. "It's booby-trapped. I'm sure of it. Remember who we're dealing with."

"Then how . . ."

But Barnes was already gone.

Ironically, it was the same cylinder Sid 6.7 had climbed by swinging up on the loose electrical cord; it seemed like years ago. Barnes pulled himself up with one easy motion and stood on the top. There was an inspection panel for a fan, held in place by three wing nuts.

Three wing nuts spun and flew off into the night.

"Hurry!" Madison Carter called out from below. Elizabeth Deane stood next to her, her bulk somehow comforting in the darkness.

"Mommy? Mommy?" Karin's voice was muffled behind the gag.

"Try and stay calm, Karin," Barnes called down, as he lifted the panel off gingerly, almost tenderly, expecting at every moment to see the flash, to feel the heat, to relive the agony of the explosion five years before.

In his memory, he heard Grimes's voice: ". . . *desperately seeking to save something he's already lost . . .*"

But there was no flash. There was just a fan, whirring in the darkness.

And underneath the fan, there she was. Karin sat bound and gagged on the floor of the cylinder, next to the low access doorway. Laser beams, like the ones Grimes had used to kill Barnes's wife and daughter, were arrayed around the door, which was connected by narrow fiber-optic cables to a bomb made of C-4 with a laptop computer as detonator. The laptop's screen was the timer. And it was counting down:

The only light other than the laptop's screen was the ON glow of the video surveillance camera that Sid 6.7 had placed halfway up the circular steel wall, taped to one of the air-conditioning coils. *A live video feed for a little girl's torture and execution.*

"What a sick bastard!" Barnes said, shaking his head. Then he thought, *How sick?* Was Sid 6.7 any sicker than the 183 humans who had gone into his composite?

Or the 18.3 million who had tuned into his "DEATH TV" show?

"Hurry!" Madison Carter called out. She could see Barnes above her, on top of the air-conditioning cylinder; he was outlined against the night sky, pulling off the fan access panel. "How much time do we have?"

"A little more than a minute," said Elizabeth Deane. She and Jack Yancey were watching an LCD television, a three-inch Watchman Deane had taken from her purse. Carter looked down at the tiny screen and was surprised to see Karin there, huddled on the other side of the door.

"She still on the TV?"

"It's nationwide," said Deane. "The networks picked up the feed. The whole country is pulling for her."

The display at the bottom of the screen read *6:31.*

6:30.

6:29.

Barnes could see the display on the laptop, counting down. He looked for a way to disconnect the fan. The motor was sealed by two large hex nuts, and with his steel-and-plastic fingers Barnes twisted until they began to spin off slowly.

6:20.

6:19.

Too slowly. Barnes gave up, and gritting his teeth—for his fiber-optic nerves transmitted a very realistic painlike sensation—he plunged his arm into the whirling blades of the fan.

KRANG!

KRANG!

KRANG!

KRA—

It stopped.

Barnes held a bent blade with his bent hand, and he twisted it up and out of the way. It had cut through his plastic "flesh" and several of the fiber-optic "nerves," rendering two fingers useless, but his plastic-and-steel "bone" was still intact.

He slipped through and hung, then dropped twelve feet to the steel floor of the cylinder, carefully avoiding the laser beams by the door. It was like being in an upright coffin.

Karin was bound and gagged on the floor.

"It's okay," Barnes said, as he untied her. Instantly, she jumped to her feet and leaped into his arms—uncovering the pressure-sensitive touchpad she'd been sitting on.

The touchpad was wired to the laptop detonator. A tiny drive whirred, and the countdown display on the laptop's screen was replaced, suddenly, by Sid 6.7's face. No longer raging, no longer furious. No longer trapped.

Cool. Sadistic. The old Sid.

Prerecorded.

"Hello, Parker," Sid 6.7 said. "That can only be you. And what should be completely clear by now, is that anything you've thought of, I've thought of first."

The countdown display reappeared in an onscreen window beside Sid 6.7's face.

5:02

5:01

"Better hustle, sport," Sid 6.7 said. "Time is running out."

His face disappeared and the countdown timer display enlarged to fill the tiny screen.

Now moving at double speed:

4:01

3:57

"Hurry!" said Karin. She was standing against the curved wall where Barnes had placed her, as still as a deer trapped in headlights.

Parker Barnes was hurrying. By moving as slowly and carefully as possible. Stepping over the laser beams, searching for the secret, the key—the way to disconnect the C-4 that was timed and primed to blow them and the roof of the building into eternity. He had to find a way. Even with the helicopter, there wasn't time to get out of the cylinder and off the building before it blew.

"Any ideas?" he called up through the bent fan blades overhead.

Madison Carter was looking down. "Type *ABORT* on the keyboard," she said.

Barnes typed ABORT.

"Now hit RETURN."

Barnes hit RETURN.

The disc drive whirred.

Sid 6.7's prerecorded face came up on the screen.

"Uh-uh-uh!" he said. "I thought of that, too. Better try again. Faster! Faster!"

The countdown display reappeared on the laptop screen. Now moving at quadruple speed:

2:51

2:43

2:35

It's in one of these wires, Barnes thought, studying the narrow fiber-optic cables connecting the laptop detonator to the vicious-looking bundle of C-4.

His glance fell to the open wound on his arm, and the broken fiber-optic "nerves" exposed in the gash.

They were the same.

Grimacing with almost-pain, he pulled six inches of yellow fiber-optic wire from his left arm, and a third finger on his left hand went dead. He held one end of the wire with his left thumb and forefinger and the other end with his right hand, studying it.

"What are you going to do?" Carter called down from above.

"Connect this side to the output—" Barnes held up the left end of the wire. "And this side to the input—" He held up the right end. "And pray."

"You mean, create an infinite feedback loop!" said Carter.

"Will it work?" asked Karin.

"Let's hope so," said Parker Barnes.

* * *

Sid 6.7 wasn't cheap.

He was a high-end killer, and he had secured a high-end laptop for his detonator. The back of the tiny computer was ported for monitors, modems, mice and joysticks, networks and displays, CDs and disc drives, input and output devices of every description.

Barnes needed only two ports. And while he was looking for them, the display on the screen was counting down at quadruple speed.

:41

:33

He inserted one end of the fiber-optic wire into OUTPUT.

He inserted the other into INPUT.

Sid 6.7's face appeared again. "Uh-uh-uh!" he said. "I thought of that, too."

"Oh, no!" said Madison, from above.

"It's not working!" cried Karin. She grabbed Barnes's hand. He squeezed it and waited for the blast.

The countdown display raced on:

:15

:08

:01

Barnes closed his eyes, waiting for the blast.

Then he opened his eyes, just in time to see the countdown display reset:

:41

:33

Sid 6.7's face reappeared on the screen. "Uh-uh-uh!" he said again. "I thought of that, too."

At Barnes's feet, the laser beams flickered and disappeared.

"Game over," he said softly, as Karin, squealing with joy, jumped up into his arms.

Barnes heard a noise and looked up. Madison was looking down through the fan, weeping.

Something struck his cheek. He tasted it with his tongue—an unfamiliar, long-forgotten, but welcome taste.

It was a tear of joy.

"Go ahead!" said Madison Carter.

This time there was no need for slowness. The laser beams were dead. The bomb disarmed.

A rescue worker cut the lock and bent down and opened the door—and Karin Carter flew out, into her mother's waiting arms.

Parker Barnes followed her out the door, also into Madison Carter's arms. He had expected, at most, a thank-you hug, and he was surprised by the kiss Carter gave him, the kind of kiss you give a man who has just saved your daughter's life.

And more for good measure.

WHUMP

WHUMP

WHUMP

"Hooray!"

Barnes looked behind him, to the spot where Madison and Karin stood with Elizabeth Deane, bathed in light. The small crowd of cops, reporters, and rescue workers who had gathered on the roof of the Multi-Media Tower were applauding and cheering. The sky was crisscrossed with the lights of TV news helicopters. The rescue had been televised coast to coast, and millions were sharing the joy and relief.

Parker Barnes felt it, too—the joy, the relief, and other new emotions he was looking forward to exploring with Karin and her mother.

But Barnes had other feelings, too. Darker feelings. Vengeance, hatred, revenge.

He let the dark feelings sweep over him, filling his heart as he walked to the edge of the building, alone and unnoticed in the darkness.

He reached into his pocket and pulled out the "SID 6.7" module. He cocked his arm, ready to fling it into the night and banish Sid 6.7 to oblivion forever.

Then a smile crossed his handsome ebony features. He had a better idea.

There are crueler fates than death.

Smiling, Barnes put the module back into his pocket and went back to join the cheering crowd.

36

THE COPTER CUT LOW, SNAKING BETWEEN THE TOWER-
ing geometric shapes of the city. The kid flying it—
and he was definitely a kid, eight years old at the
most—handled the joystick expertly, soaring between
the crystalline towers.

"Johnny!" said another boy, coming up behind
him. "Forget that crummy old thing. You're up. It's
your turn on the new game!"

Johnny dropped the joystick and turned away from
the video game. The helicopter crashed into the side
of a skyscraper as the two boys ran to the front of the
arcade.

Johnny cut through the crowd of boys and girls
gathered around the new arcade game. "Awesome!"
he exclaimed as he picked up the VR pistol—an
oversize .50 Desert Eagle, like the gun Schwarzeneg-
ger used in the old movies.

Johnny picked up his VR goggles and stepped to the
center of a small arena, surrounded by big-screen
monitors. The monitors all showed the same scene—

a broken-down upright piano half-buried in a sand dune, a water fountain tipped over on its side, a phone booth with a scruffy crow on top.

Johnny dropped in two quarters and slipped his VR goggles down over his eyes. His figure came up on the screen—a fierce futuristic gladiator.

"Go, Johnny, go!" cried the crowd of watching kids.

The credits rolled:

SID STALKER
Starring SID 2.1
Copyright, P. Barnes.

Johnny's adversary walked out from behind the piano—a scruffy little man with gleaming white teeth, dressed like a cross between a cowboy and a prospector. He had bright blue eyes and dirty blond hair. He looked tired for a cartoon character. The look in his eyes was stupid and sad.

Strapped to Sid 2.1's waist was an ancient, rusty .22. "Ready to draw, pardner?" Sid 2.1 asked, his voice a little slow, a little flat.

Johnny nodded. His figure on the screen nodded.

"This one," Sid 2.1 said in a slow, whining monotone, "is for me."

Sid 2.1 drew. But Johnny squeezed off three shots before Sid 2.1's gun cleared his holster. Sid 2.1 fell, pieces of his face blown away. He tried to get up. Johnny fired again.

And again.

The crow squawked.

CONGRATULATIONS read the display. THE WORLD IS NOW SAFE FOR ANOTHER DAY.

"My turn! My turn!" said twenty small voices at once.